DESERT CHILD

Also by Simon Parke:

DESERT ASCENT
or
A Brief History of Eternity

Desert Child

or

Just How Amusing
Can a Nightmare Be?

Simon Parke

Hodder & Stoughton
LONDON   SYDNEY   AUCKLAND

British Library Cataloguing in Publication Data:
A record for this book is available from the British Library.

ISBN 0 340 69412 2

Typeset in Monotype Columbus by
Strathmore Publishing Services, London N7.

Printed and bound in Great Britain by
Mackays of Chatham PLC
Chatham, Kent

Hodder and Stoughton Ltd
A division of Hodder Headline PLC
338 Euston Road, London NW1 3BH

Thank you to Hodders, whose faith and hope may be rewarded in heaven. They certainly won't be on earth.

Thank you to Albert Lubin, who understood the stranger on the earth better than me.

Thank you to Harry, for facing the stranger's question.

Thank you to Chloë, for bringing him home in the first place.

Thank you to Joy, for reading the manuscript and even ticking occasionally. A tick from her goes a long way. Across eternity, in fact.

The book is dedicated to all who have loved and lost, and, amidst the river of pain running through them, are trying to love again.

Contents

Introduction

EVERYONE loves a list. You know where you are with a list. A shopping list. A list of the top hundred best-selling singles of all time. A list of the things which need to be done before you go on holiday. Top five box-office films from 1973. The twenty most important inventions in history. The thousand richest people on planet earth. The seven fattest American presidents. Lists sort things. Settle things. Settle arguments. Settle minds. Clarify. Bring order.

Or rather, some lists do. Other lists? Well, others, try as they might, they don't clarify anything at all. Not a bean. Apart from madness, of course, but madness isn't clarifying. It's just mad. And this, for good or ill – probably ill – is a story about such lists. It's about lists which sort out absolutely nothing. Publisher's nightmare. But then what can you expect from lists which come from the desert?

I really had no desire to edit more desert diaries. As you may or may not know, I've been down this path before. But when the desert diary of Jenny came my way, with its marvellous set of consumer-unfriendly lists, the lure was just irresistible. Vanity, as ever. I have a keen eye for failure, and a track record to die for in this department. So why should someone else grab the credit for this particular disaster? No. This *Titanic* was *mine*.

I needed to do a little extra research to fill out the story. Interviews in the sun. It's a hard life. I've inserted this additional material into Jenny's own narrative where I felt appropriate. Otherwise, it's Jenny's story. And the lists, of course. It was her opinion that some lists are more important than others. Whether these were them, I'm not sure. But then I'm not paid to have opinions. I'm just the messenger. And here beginneth the message ...

Simon Parke
Pentecost 1997

Prologue

THE earth stopped revolving for a moment in shock as the two men considered the implications of the words just spoken; as the two men felt the fall-out from the bombshell just lobbed into the conversation. The visitor spoke first.

'Now that is a very revolutionary thought, my friend.'

'A supremely dangerous muttering, yes, I know. Very dangerous. Not uttered lightly. I was hesitant even as I spoke. The story of the Church has so often been a convincing win for rhetoric over reality. And I really don't want to add to the nonsense. As our Buddhist friends so wisely warn, "Don't sell too intoxicating a liquor."'

'Of course. But nevertheless, you think the – er – revolution possible?'

'Well, I feel that it is, yes.'

'Awe-inspiring. Quite awe-inspiring. Imagine it.'

'Sometimes I do, believe me. And it's wonderful.'

The two men smiled at each other, sharing the dangerous secret, and walked on until they reached a large door which said Refectory. They were both still clearly in a state of shock.

'Best not to run before we can walk though,' said the host, eager to calm the almost revivalist fervour unleashed between them.

'Absolutely not. One step at a time.'

'Very important, yes. And the first step at this particular time, is, I think, tea.'

'Tea. Very good. Tea should precede every revolution.'

They gazed up through the sky to the universe beyond. It was the visitor who spoke.

'You know something?'

'What?'

'I feel Satan quaking already …'

CHAPTER ONE

Cracks

'WHAT is it that you want?' asked a large bearded man in a black dress.

He should have known better. He really should. I mean, *please!* I'd just climbed a thousand cruddy steps in appalling heat. I was entitled to respect. They hadn't just been exhausting. They'd been dangerous. Cracked by ice; dislodged by rain; baked stupid by sun and unrepaired since the days when Adam's grandfather was just a lad, these steps gave desert misery a bad name. In the sketches I'd studied before leaving, they'd appeared as neat, dainty, tidy and very *nayce*. Travel brochure shite. They were lethal. Crumbling, disintegrating, worn, slippery, and tortuous. And then half way up, someone's had the nerve the build a little arch with a cross carved on it, asking me to confess my sins

3

as I stoop low to continue my journey. They wished. They didn't know Jenny Jewel. I'm not sure I did, either, but that's beside the point.

'What is it that you want?' The large bearded man in black with a ridiculous head-covering repeated his question, as my weary eyes spun in the sun. This was not home territory. I was floundering.

'A medal, I think. Joke. Attempt at humour. Does that sort of thing go on in the desert?'

Apparently not. Amusing asides had clearly been outlawed in these parts some while ago. He just stared at me, half-smiling but clearly waiting for a serious reply. What was I doing here?

I'd kept to the one-rucksack rule, but with the camera as well, it added up. It particularly added up when walking up Mount Sinai. It hadn't been a long drive from Sharm el-Sheik airport in the jeep. But it had been basic and startling. The pock-marked, rock-strewn desert landscape, dominated by the huge mountains, gave no sense of welcome. The scenery, in fact, had the social skills of a rather graceless alien, and seemed to be saying only: this is the moon. From here on, earth rules don't apply ...

And then a very long climb up a large number of steps and another alien in a skirt opens the door of this strange lunar settlement and asks me what it is that I want. Well, I think there's only one answer to that. I want to go home, thank you very much. I want to call back the jeep, driven by that nice man from the Muzeina bedouin tribe, all robes and trainers, and ask him if he might turn round and take me back to Sharm el-Sheik airport, and yes thank you, I'd enjoyed my desert trip very much indeed, and I would most certainly be back, and I would most certainly be asking for his services again when I did return. But I couldn't do that, as my camera reminded me. Not yet.

'Everything.' I said. 'All right? Will that do? What is it that I want? I want everything. And I want it with icing. Plenty of icing. And a cherry. A large one. And I want it before tomorrow evening if that's OK with the rest of the universe.'

'Certainly,' said the alien, 'I think you'll find the universe very open to that idea.'

Not my universe.

'Very open indeed. You want everything, plus the icing, plus the cherry? Very good. The desert is just the place to be ambitious. What with the faraway so close.'

'Sorry?'

'The faraway so close.'

'Ah.'

Why did I ask? What was the point? Why didn't I just leave it? My arms were sore with carrying, my throat parched, my legs dull with ache. I shouldn't have given a damn. But for some reason I was still interested to know what the hell he was talking about. Despite the beard, the dress and the stupid hat. Despite the fact that earth rules clearly meant nothing here. And despite the fact that he was a man and in all likelihood, therefore, not talking about anything at all.

'The faraway so close. It's why *I* came here. You said you wanted everything. Well, the faraway so close – it's my version of everything. Everything I wanted. To grasp the faraway, and to know it close.'

'Could I just suggest something?'

'Certainly,' he said.

'Please don't try and understand me,' I said. 'And please don't give me *your* version of what I'm trying to say. We'll get on much better that way. We're not the same, you and I. Not the same at all. For one thing, I'm from planet earth. And for another thing, I'm not a believer and have nil desire to become one. Me and believing don't go. Or rather we do, but in separate directions. I'm here on business.'

He smiled.

'So what is it that you want?' he asked again.

Bloody hell! This man was beginning to get on my nerves.

Well, I did want everything. But failing that – and I

was failing pretty badly so far – failing that, a good programme would do for starters. I wanted to make a good programme. A Critics' Choice. I'd come to this God-forsaken holy place stuck on a mountain which seemed to go on forever, to take a wry, amusing and slightly sideways look at shrines around the world. Last month, Buddha's birthplace in Nepal. This month, St Raphael's set on Mount Sinai, with its very own burning bush. *Blackpool, it isn't* was our working title, and the series would hopefully run in the autumn schedules if it wasn't ousted by a wry, amusing and slightly sideways American sitcom.

'I wouldn't mind being let in,' I replied.

'Yes, but what is it you want?'

After my journey so far, I wanted a nice man to give me a cup of tea and then leave me alone with a footbath while he took my load to my very comfortable room, only to return when he had news of the large meal awaiting me. Dream on.

'I mean, which party are you with?'

Which party was I with? Was there a choice? It seemed an unlikely venue for a lager-soaked *partyfest*.

'Which group?'

Which group? Hey, I was with no group. I was independent, me. Jenny Jewel, the stand-up comic, slayer of multi-nationals and only occasionally forced to do adverts for them, when there were cash-flow problems. Ten years on the alternative comedy circuit, no one owned me. Apart from my building society, of course.

'The psychologists are in the west wing, the scientists in the east, the day-trippers in the main courtyard and the retreatants in the annex. Who are you with?'

Arriving at monasteries was not the simple exercise I'd imagined it would be. I hadn't really considered the possibility of there being hard, searching and largely incomprehensible questions like 'What is it that you want?' and 'Who are you with?' on arrival. I'd spent most of my preparation time working out my wardrobe. How many of everything? And what colour? Would have to go with monastery walls. Cream might be safest. Make-up? My Avon lady had been to Greece last year for her holidays but felt uncomfortable about what would be best for the desert. She didn't get a lot of people asking what happened to eye-liner on Sinai.

And washing facilities? Did monks wash their clothes? If they did, would I want to use the same washing machine? Best to allow for no washing facilities and take two weeks' worth of clothes. And toiletries. Again, I'd felt it best to assume nothing. Assume the last Boots was in Dover, and go prepared.

'I'm here to do some filming. I'm making a documentary, and so I'm not knowingly either a scientist, psychologist, day-tripper or retreatant.'

'You don't really fit in, do you?' said beardy man with a smile.

'Funny you should say that,' I said. 'You aren't the first.'

'Follow me,' he said.

'Generally, I loathe large bearded men who assume I'm going to do what they say. But I'll make an exception in your case.'

'How fortunate,' he said, 'because it's either that, or a very long walk back down the steps you've just climbed and a slightly uncertain future in the beautiful but decidedly inhospitable arid wastes beyond.'

Bastard.

'My name's Merrybum,' he continued. 'Novice Merrybum.'

Merrybum? Was this a Carry-On film? *Carry-On up the Mountain*? 'Ooh-er, missus, and mind my innuendo – I just can't keep it down!' Merrybum. This must be the moon. Still, it was quite entertaining. A name full of cracks, you might say, and my mind was instantly buzzing with Happy Bottom and Cheery Arse jokes. Cheeky, cheeky! Little did he know the funfair which was breaking out in my mind.

'Lends itself to cracks, doesn't it?'

'Sorry?'

'It's a name full of cracks. People usually start with that one.'

'Do they? I hadn't really – '

'And then the cheeky-cheeky jokes, of course.'

'That's not my style. I'm not a child, you know.'

'Of course not. And by all means call me Happy Bottom or Cheery Arse in the privacy of your own room, but to my face, Merrybum would be appreciated.'

'That's fine. No problem. Pretty normal name, as it goes. I prefer to judge people on who they are, not what they're called,' I said, with quiet shame and incriminating sweat trickling down my back.

'Greatly appreciated.'

'Fine. I'm cool to that. Whatever.'

I sensed a chip on his shoulder. I was looking for some vinegar to apply.

Overlooked by Mount Sinai, we walked. We walked past some outhouses; we walked past what looked like a minaret but obviously couldn't be; we walked past a big shrub which looked slightly lost; and we walked past more bearded men in dresses. Or robes, as they suddenly become in the religious context. For all its fame, I didn't sense that St Raphael's was exactly dripping with investment. It all felt pretty sparse, pretty basic and just very very old. Without wishing to state the obvious, this place had been here a long time.

'Yours must be a pretty bleak life though, if, as you say, you *greatly appreciate* being called Merrybum; if someone calling you Merrybum is somehow integral to a good day.'

'Life is bleak,' he said calmly, 'very bleak,' and strode on ahead of me.

He was right, of course. More right than he could possibly know in this desert ivory tower. And I sensed then that the making of this amusing documentary on St Raphael's wasn't going to turn out quite as wry and quirky as I'd hoped. They say life hugs the Nile. But death hugs the desert beyond. And right now, we were somewhere beyond the beyond. Quite *how* far beyond became apparent later that evening.

★

I was looking for a toilet, and there was a sense of urgency in my search. So, in the absence of a policeman, I asked a day-tripper. Someone had said there was one round the corner. 'You'll find it.' But I never did. Round the corner I was faced with three doors, and a rather surprised rat making for cover. I chose the door furthest from the rat's exit. I pushed and it opened. I walked into an enclosed darkness. A room or a corridor? I was feeling for the light switch when the gradual outline of a candle on the wall became apparent. No matches. I stumbled on. It was like a cathedral cloister.

All arches, stone floor and dark corners. Suddenly a noise, something smashing, and a swift movement near my feet. I was completely freaked. It was another rat. The place was clearly infested. I bent down to pick up the broken crockery. Only it wasn't. It was smooth, in a slightly rough sort of way. Odd shapes. But with night vision coming into play, I could see where it had fallen from, for there was a pile of similar shapes up against the wall. My heart was pounding so much I could have been in an Enid Blyton adventure. I hated this. And then I saw. Realised. And my pounding heart almost stopped. I preferred it pounding. They were skulls. Oh, my God. There was a huge pile of skulls in here. Hundreds of them, literally. I was standing in a dark, rat-invested cloister with a large pile of skulls. I cracked, wet my knickers and began to cry. I knelt and sobbed. Not caring now, not caring, but caring very much, painfully so, and why does life have to be so awful, and then the match striking, the candle being lit, a figure in the darkness, a figure holding a candle and moving towards me, and I thought, oh no – not another beard-ed man in black, finding me like this, not like this, go away, I just want to be left alone, I don't want to see you, I don't like bearded men in black …

But it wasn't. It wasn't a bearded man. It was a woman. A nun. Slight, wrinkled, old. Everything a nun should be, of course. Pleated skirt. Round, stooped, custom-built humble shoulders. She'd appeared from nowhere, and more particularly from a small door at the far end. And I loved her. Loved her before she opened her mouth. She had rescued me. And she wasn't a bearded man.

'I thought I heard something.'

'I'm lost.'

'You better come with me.'

I would have stepped off the edge of the planet with her at that particular moment. Being saved is so brilliant because being lost and scared is so awful. I followed her through the door at the far end, and up a little winding staircase, into a medium-sized room with the blinds down, a bed in the corner, a worn mat carpet and a sink with some large taps, one of which dripped. Nothing else.

'My name's Rowena and I don't really exist.'

'I see,' I lied.

CHAPTER TWO

Blackpool, It Isn't

I did my first take the following day. There was no budget for a sound crew, make-up artist, choreographer. As for a best boy, chance would have been a fine thing. I would have settled for a half-decent boy, frankly. I'd given up waiting for my prince to come, you see. Since Chris. No men. But that was another story. In the meantime, I was building a career. This was a good job. Lots of celebs doing quirky travelogues these days. Just them, alone with nature – and a film crew of four thousand. But I'd have to do it all by myself, all on my own-some. As in filming, so in life. But I could handle it. After all, the first programme in the series had been filmed at Lourdes during the rush-hour, with pilgrims streaming forward from all directions, and when death by crutch or wheelchair is a real danger. In fact, they say that it's more dangerous to be healed at Lourdes than it is to drive in a slightly uncertain fashion along an Italian motorway. So St Raphael's shouldn't present too many problems. I'd survived Lourdes. And no one got healed here as far as I knew.

The day-trippers were numerous and might have been a problem. They had three hundred a day, so I was told. But they weren't interested in me. Thus I wasn't bothered by gormless young people with their banners saying 'Hello mum' in the background. They all had their own travel videos to make anyway, with their own rather better equipment. Some, of course, were still grumbling about the large blue shawls they had to wear to make themselves 'decent'. After all, the implications for the body-beautiful-wannabees were serious. No one was really saying it, but I could see them all thinking it, because I was thinking it too: if you *had* to visit a holy place, you might at least have a good tan to show for it. Otherwise, what's the point of a holy place, frankly?

Meanwhile, no sign yet of the mysterious psychologists and scientists, and as for the retreatants, well – the only image I had in my mind was the Hunchback of Notre Dame. Huddled. Stooped. Broken. And pretty damn desperate. Not my sort. Too busy dribbling confession and repentance and beating themselves with sticks to be bothered with me.

'Hullo,' he said.

'Hullo.'

He was a big man with a kind smile, in some cheap and slightly ill-fitting jeans. His shirt was just too small for him, and the buttons were in pain.

'You look like someone who is thrustingly famous doing something enormously interesting,' he said.

Was he taking the piss?

'I'm making a series of programmes about famous religious shrines around the world.'

'Ah. Well, take back what I said about doing something enormously interesting.'

'And who are you?'

'Oh, no one really. Desert flotsam. Honours degree in failure, and cracked both by age and general disapproval. But strangely happy, actually – happy to be wandering about this morning with nothing and no one making demands on me. And enjoying meeting you, of course. Saw you arrive.'

'So you're not a scientist or a psychologist?'

'God forbid.'

'A day-tripper?'

'Please!'

'So you're a, er, retreatant?'

'I suppose so. But you don't need to move away quite so obviously. It's not contagious. You can't catch it from lavatory seats.'

And that was my first meeting with Peter. It wasn't to be my last.

★

'*Blackpool, it isn't*, take one: In the blazing bone-dry heat of the desert, some things die an instant death. Chocolate absent-mindedly left in the pocket, for instance. But other things seem to last for ever. Like monasteries. They seem to take the melting heat as a personal challenge to last for bloody ages. Which is exactly what St Raphael's has managed. Set on Mount Sinai, where God cut out the naughty bits all those years ago with the Ten Commandments, it's been here since 550 AD, the proud creation of the Emperor Justinian. Blackpool, it isn't, but if you like getting up at 4 a.m. to intone a three-hour service; feel the personal need of no less than ten chapels, several thousand icons, and can bear the freezing winter mornings as well as the mosquitoes in the summer, then this place may very well be for you. Wish you were here?' (Quirky grin.)

I paused, upped sticks, and decided to display a little of the fruit of my pre-travel research. I was standing in front of the large plant I'd passed on arrival, leafy and quite as tall as me.

'*Blackpool, it isn't*, take two: Well, it may look like just another shrub to you, but on a good day it sets light to itself and talks to anyone foolish enough to listen. Yes, this is, supposedly, the original burning bush.'

I made a great play of taking my shoes off. And then, in a whisper to the camera:

'Well, we don't want to upset the management, do we! Yes, when Moses came here originally it was definitely shoes-off time. And of course, despite all his protestations, this plant promptly sent him to Egypt to lead the Israelites to freedom. Imagine being sent to a foreign country by a vegetable. The vegetable who sent me is called David and he's my producer ...'

I was still getting my bearings. Still feeling for the place. I'd change all this. Rework the material. Sharpen up the gags. But it seemed important to get under way. And equally important that the material was as much about me as the place, of course. The idea was that these holy places should be a vehicle for me. Jenny Jewel does Lourdes. This should be a gas! Jenny Jewel does Buddha's birthplace! What a hoot! Jenny Jewel meets the burning bush. This I *must* see! After twenty-four hours on site, it was also good to get into territory where I felt confident. The camera. The scripted word. Tools of the trade and the trade was control. Control, control. Nothing quite like it for calming the soul.

*

'What is it that you want?'

'I just want you to hear me out, Archbishop.'

'I have heard you out, Ted. Now, unfortunately, you've come back in again.'

'This is a better offer, my final offer as it goes, and

one which is going to save this God-forsaken relic of a building from extinction. You know it and I know it. And you know that I know it. And I know that you know it.'

'Well aren't we all so knowledgeable. How exactly were you getting home?'

Unfortunately, the camera wasn't rolling, because this would have fitted in nicely at the top of the programme. Two men, antlers locked, contesting territory. Despite the chapels, the prayer, the icons and the talking bush, all was apparently not well at St Raphael's. There was a cancer in the cloisters, pus in the pews. Archbishop Musselly, who ran the community, was having a slight disagreement with an entrepreneur from Cairo called Ted Delbaba. I had just called for my first interview with the Archbishop, when Ted had knocked on the door. I'd made to leave, but the Arch had said I could stay, that he wouldn't be long. I'd last encountered Ted in Putney selling double-glazing. Or someone very like him.

'You know what happened in Jericho, Archbishop,' said Ted.

'The walls fell down, yes.'

'They bloody did, and all. Round and round the garden like a teddy bear, atishoo, atishoo, we all fall down, as far as I remember. And it's going to happen here, only without the atishoo and without trumpets. And the, er, teddies.'

I'm no bible scholar, but even I was sensing a slight mix-up of stories here.

'You know what the salt water is doing to the foundations,' continued the Putney-double.

'I know exactly what the salt water is doing to our foundations, Ted. It's rotting them. It's eating away at the granite. It's threatening this monastery in a way that the sun has never been able to,' said Arch with feeling.

'Bleeding tragedy, eh? So famous and all that, so old, so holy, yet with all the future of a Nissen hut with a cracked roof. Terrible shame.'

'A challenge, certainly.'

'You'll be the laughing stock, won't you? That'll be a good one for your CV. Doesn't bear thinking about.'

'Then don't tax yourself with the worry. We'll face it, and we'll deal with it, without resorting to help from some sick soul like yourself who wants to make a millennium prostitute out of us.'

'You can't look reality in the face, can you?'

'I'm trying to, but you keep getting in the way.'

'You don't realise. You don't realise the game you're in . You haven't the first bleeding clue. You're sitting on a potential goldmine here, and all you want to do is sit in a chapel and say 'Let us pray.' You are being offered two million by my consortium. That's two million pounds! And suddenly atishoo, atishoo, the walls *don't* all fall down thank you very much because Archbishop Musselly has got off his backside, raised some dough and *sorted* it. Sorted the salt water that's going to destroy it all.'

'I will sort it. Believe me, I will. But I'll sort you first.'

'Was that a threat?'

'Or was it a prophecy? Very hard to tell the difference sometimes. I'll leave you to make up your own mind. No hurry. But in the meantime do me, the angels and the archangels a favour – and leave.'

'I'm your salvation, Archbishop.'

'Not in the orthodox creeds, you aren't.'

'I'm your lifeline.'

'A depressing thought. And one barely strong enough to cling to the sound waves which link us.'

Archbishop Musselly was as broad as he was tall. He was compact. He was a tank with a crew cut. I could imagine him doing two hundred press-ups before moving on to the proper exercise. It wasn't a turn on for me. I preferred my men slightly effete; strangers to the gym and all the absurd posturing which accompanies it. But when it did all come to a head, when it all finally exploded, it was very spectacular. When the prophecy was fulfilled, and the sorting undertaken, it was all very spectacular indeed. Great TV. I only got there at the end, of course, and by that time more TV footage wasn't uppermost in my mind.

'Imagine it, Archbishop. It's the millennium morning, all right? Can you picture it?'

Ted was the patient teacher, having one last go at explaining to young Musselly a very basic idea which the rest of the class had got ages ago. He had sat himself in the Archbishop's swivel chair, put his feet on the Archbishop's desk and pretended Mr Nice Guy, Mr Reasonable.

'It's the millennium morning and the whole world is a bloody TV studio, isn't it? Course it is. Cameras everywhere trying to 'define the moment' as we say in the trade. They're all trying to get the definitive shot. And where are most of them? Where are most of the cameras, film crews, sound units, and location catering lorries? Pissing about on Chatham Islands, five hundred miles east of New Zealand. Sunrise 3.59 a.m., January 1st, in the two thousandth year of our Lord.'

'Let's not bring our Lord into the millennium, Ted. Please.'

'But us? We don't want to be on Chatham Islands, do we? We don't even want to be on Concorde trying to catch *three* millennium sunrises. We want to be *here*. Yep. Course we do. Right here, matey. On your doorstep.

In your front room. In your face.'

'In your dreams.'

'Holy Dawn Productions wants to be on Mount Sinai,' continued Ted. 'We want to bring the *religious* dimension to it all.'

'You were outbid for Chatham Islands, under your former name of First Millennium Morning Productions; you also lost out in the race for the Three Sunrises under your new name of Three Millennium Morning Productions; and so suddenly you're Holy Dawn Productions and we're meant to be impressed? Grateful even.'

'It saddens my heart to see a religious leader so cynical. A sad commentary on the times we live in, I suppose. But believe me –'

'Very difficult, Ted.'

'Believe me, we are giving you the pulpit of your dreams.'

'I *never* dream of pulpits.'

'Tell me, Archbishop, have you ever spoken, personally, to the world? Not to a few waifs and strays who've staggered here in God knows what sort of a shape. But to the world. To hundreds and millions of people. Because that's who'll be watching with us on the millennium morning. Who could resist it? Place of the Commandments. The burning bush. The crossroads of the three major monotheistic religions, Christianity, Islam and er –'

'Judaism?'

'That as well, yep. We'll be right here. Giving the holy angle. We've already got a team working on the ten *new* commandments. The old ones obviously need updating.'

'Obviously.'

'Ten new commandments for the next millennium. You'll be more famous than Jesus, two million pounds better off, and the crumbling granite dealt with for another thousand years, by which time you and me, matey, will be away with the pharaohs, and a very long way from giving a toss, if you'll 'scuse my French. Two million pounds for nothing and a congregation the like of which you've never even dreamt of. Sounds like a pretty good morning's work. I have here all the necessary paperwork. All it requires is a signature. Simple, eh?'

'Was it Richard III who lamented seeming a saint when most he played the devil?'

'I wouldn't know. Not my department, that,' said the devil.

'No.'

'Face your fear, Archbishop. Face your fear about the future. Everyone's afraid sometime.'

Musselly was by the window. He looked long at Ted.

'Do you know how much I fear, Ted?' he said. 'This is how much I fear.'

He held his fist against the glass, contemplating them both. Then he looked at Ted. And then, still looking at Ted, he smashed his fist through the glass. There was blood amidst the splinters, but not the amount of blood there would have been if a main artery had been slashed. He'd live this time. Musselly used a handkerchief for a tourniquet.

'That's how much I fear, Ted.'

Ted was thrown, edgy, wanting out.

'You're a crazy man, Archbishop, off your head, but I'll tell you this. It's my final offer and the decision is yours. So I'll leave you and your party tricks, I'll leave you with your angels and your archangels to have a little chat amongst yourselves. And when, after much prayer and fasting, you finally say yes, please don't give it a holy spin. Please don't say you feel led or guided, or any bull like that. Because you're no different. No different to the rest of us. Like the rats in the sewer, the flies on the dung and the pimps in Bangkok, like the rest of us, you just want to survive. You just want to continue, and you'll do all things necessary. When it comes to the wire, you'll seize the chance, praying your way to the bank and to hell with the consequences.'

Cut. But as I say, unfortunately, I didn't have the camera.

*

'I'd like you to *feel* that leather in your soul,' said the pervert in the library. 'Feel it. Feel the orgasm of antiquity in the very core of your being. Feel it explode. Feel it all over you. Feel it pressing against your body, caressing you. Antiquity. It is a lover. A dangerous lover and your defences are down, your boundaries melting, and your psyche invaded. Ahhh! This holy library. It is a brothel of sensual and aesthetic experience ...'

Fr Lopez, our guide, was getting very excited indeed, but I'm not sure anyone else was. The lover in question was an old book of prayers from the vast library at St Raphael's and I was part of the tour party. High ceiling and dripping with gold paint, it was in severe contrast to the rest of the buildings. Most of the group seemed to be a set of English Christians from the south coast doing the Timeless Nile and Beyond trip with the Lord is my Shepherd travel firm. The others were Japanese. The Japanese translator, however, was struggling with some of Lopez' imagery. She had probably been preparing for this tour by mugging up on *Archaeology Today* and *History Monthly*. The *Kama Sutra* would have been more appropriate. Lopez was a man in love with the sense, sight, smell, touch and feel of history, beauty and symbol. He was a man in love with his artefacts. And the pressing question was: how far can you go?

'Herodotus? This book was my first mistress here. Has anyone here read Herodotus?'

No one had.

'And the *Histories* of Thucydides? These are the *Histories* of Thucydides in one scrolled volume.'

He was in awe.

'Here. Take it.'

He lovingly passed the scrolls to one of the south coast Christians. She was holding it with some reluctance and some fear.

'How does it feel, madam? Run your fingers over it and tell me how it feels. Tell me if antiquity makes you quiver.'

The woman ran her fingers across the scroll rather half-heartedly and said that yes, it was very nice.

'I must confess,' said Lopez, 'that I have often pressed that scroll against my inner thigh.'

The woman dropped the scroll, as if it was the dung of a rabid dog. Smack it went, on stone floor, and Lopez died of shock and then rose again in trauma to pick it up, dust it down and tend generally to its every need. The emotional and psychic energy in the monastery library at that moment could have lit Manhattan for ten days. A Strict Baptist from Bournemouth tried to calm the whole thing down at this point by asking if the library had been digitally photographed and made available to scholars on the Internet. Fr Lopez, like a man interrupted in the course of making love, acknowledged in a rather uninterested way that this was indeed a goal of Archbishop Musselly, but clearly it was not one shared by him. It can be bloody awkward holding a computer terminal against your inner thigh and something less than sensual, I could see that.

We'd already done the religious bits. The garments, gowns, furniture and fittings acquired by fifteen hundred years of intense religion. So we'd seen the sacred vessels, the chalice and diskos for the bread and wine; the censer for the incense; the container for the holy oil; and the blessing cross – carved wood inside a silver-gilt frame with semi-precious stones.

But Fr Lopez had really upped a gear when he got on to the vestments. The holy clothes. The soft cloth of the *Epigonation*, worn by the priest suspended from the waist, was a particular delight to him. In the twelfth century, it was meant to symbolise the towel which Jesus used to wash the disciples' feet. By the fifteenth century, it had somehow also become a symbol of the Resurrection. By the twentieth century, in the hands of the pervert Lopez, who knows what it meant? And then he was into the *Epanikia*, the long cuffs on the lower part of the priest's sleeves, which had started out life as just being very handy at baptisms, and ended up as symbolising the fetters which bound Christ when brought before the High Priest Caiaphas. It was about now that I'd first noticed the Strict Baptist from Bournemouth beginning to sweat, and it wasn't the heat. For myself, I was quite enjoying it. We all need something to give us a spring in our step, and right now, with Fr Lopez exuding, we were listening to a very well-sprung man indeed.

And then Novice Merrybum was beside me saying that Archbishop Mussely was going to be delayed due to the disappearance of little.

'A little what?' I asked.

'Little. That's her name.'

'Who's name?'

'Little's name.'

'There's someone called Little?'

'Yes.'

'And they've disappeared?'

'Yes.'

'And who *is* Little?'

'We're not sure,' he said. 'And that isn't her name.'

Fine. So that's cleared that one up, then.

★

Rowena poured some desert tea. The blinds were still down and I was glad. This was an important space for me. A safe place. A place where I didn't feel I was working. I knew that because I hadn't even thought to bring the camera. And where I didn't feel I was in opposition to anyone either. The vague sense of 'me against them', which had been twisting my shoulder and neck muscles for most of my life, with only occasional relief from a masseur – I didn't feel it here. I don't mind life being a struggle. I was used to that. But if sometimes it isn't – well, that's a good place to be. This wasn't a massage. But it was the best I could hope for here. And it was cool. A cool corner in the blast furnace which is the desert.

'I suppose I'm here because I've done two very unnatural things in my life,' she said.

She paused. She was demanding that I ask, before she continued.

'And what are those?'

'Do you want to know?'

'Yes.'

'Why?'

Why? Because I'm nosy, that's why. Stupid question, you daft old bat.

'I'm interested, I suppose,' said I maturely and reflectively. 'Interested to know what brings anyone to a place like this. What brings a woman to a place like this.'

Gender issue. Nice one.

'You don't feel much, do you?' she said.

'Sorry?'

'You think much but you don't feel much. Or rather you do – but the feelings are buried deep, and too dangerous to let out, probably. So your initial reaction in life is to be interested but not involved. Life is interesting but not ultimately involving.'

Pause. She'd suddenly do this. Pause. Vacuum. With the expectation that muggins here would fill it, fill the gap, but muggins wasn't going to. This saviour was beginning to irritate me. So she, like me, had the latest pop psycho-babble book for Christmas. But she needn't practise on me. They were fun, of course, these books, but only meant to entertain family and friends till the New Year, when real life could start again. My copy had reached the toilet shelf now. After a six-month stay there it would duly make its way to the Oxfam shop and be reunited in the book rack with all its brothers and sisters who it grew up with in the publisher's warehouse.

'From Confusion to Identity. That's the First of the Five Paths of Mysticism.'

'I'm not really into that.'

'No. Quite understand.'

She busied herself with setting a mousetrap.

'Doesn't stop it being true, of course,' she continued, as she placed the goat's cheese on the spike. 'But as you say, it's a truth you're not into yet. One that you haven't discovered for yourself. The Five Paths of Mysticism are there, true and crucial for your growth and wholeness. But as you say, you're choosing to ignore them at the moment. Fair enough. After all, who wants a path when you can rip yourself to pieces in the surrounding under-growth? Quite.'

The mousetrap was placed beneath the sink.

'Forgive me, but I've given up releasing the little treasures back into the wild. I've discovered they think this *is* the wild.'

I smiled.

'It's the movement, of course, towards some sort of self-understanding. The First Path. From Confusion to Identity. Towards some sort of self-awareness.'

'Self-awareness?'

'Yes. Do you have a problem with that?'

'No.'

'It feels like you do. You're all locked up around the jaw.'

'No, it was just that I thought this was Mount Sinai, Middle East, but apparently not. Still, if this is Mount Sinai, California I can live with that.'

'The Middle East is the cradle of self-awareness.'

'So what is it exactly – apart from a load of tosh?'

'"Awareness means the capacity to see a coffee pot and hear the birds sing in one's own way, and not the way one was taught."'

'Very nice, I'm sure.'

'Can be very painful, but it has its uses in helping you to discern some of the cross-currents that fight within you. Old, deep and surging currents which render you very helpless sometimes, and leave you feeling like a dull echo of your parents. Still, I'm sure those cross-currents can enjoy their slightly restless co-existence within you for a while longer. I'm *sure* they can. Well, they'll have to, won't they!' she added with a beaming smile, 'because, as you say, you're not into that.'

'You didn't answer my question,' I said.

'Which question was that?'

'Your unnatural activities.'

'Ah, yes. I was telling you about my unnatural life. I buried both my children.'

I was slightly thrown.

'Yes, I'd call that unnatural, wouldn't you? Little darlings. I should have passed the baton of existence on to them and then dropped out of the race. It should have been me being lowered into the grave. Not them. But it wasn't to be. Instead, it was they who dropped out of the race and me who staggered on. I outlived them. My children were asked to give the baton back to me. That isn't natural.'

There were tears in her eyes, but to my shame, my first question was a technical one, but one which happened to interest me.

'Can nuns have children, then?'

She paused. Sighed. And looked very small.

'Apparently not. Not into old age anyway …'

CHAPTER THREE

Little Known

'So it's an annual event, is it, this feast?' I asked.
'Yes,' replied Merrybum. 'It's been going and indeed growing for ten years or so now.'

'And the aim?'

'To keep religion in touch with the latest developments in science and psychology.'

'Hence the three-day invasion of biologists, chemists, physicists, mathematicians, astronomers, psychologists, psychoanalysts, behaviourists et al?'

'Yes. It *is* a bit of a do, I grant you. But worth it. It is important to meet together and eat.'

'Wouldn't it be cheaper and much easier on the catering staff just to have their articles and books flown out occasionally?'

'It would, but there would be no profit. It is in the human encounter that truth lies. Not in the printed exchange of ideas. We are people, not thought boxes.'

Not true. Bones Jones, my physics teacher, was just a thought box. He had never managed to be a person.

If an emotion ever entered the room, he'd tend to turn to the white board and scribble something like $E=mc^2$, in the firm belief that Einstein's seminal equation concerning his theory of special relativity would somehow exorcise the danger.

'And do you seriously think that all these scientists are equally interested in catching up on the latest developments in religion?'

'Of course not, but we do find they tend to be deeply committed to a free holiday in the sun without the family in tow. Why does anyone ever go on a conference?'

'Cynic.'

'And some *are* interested. And many believe, of course. This whole science versus religion thing is largely the invention of the media. Forty per cent of scientists in America have a personal belief in God anyway which, interestingly, is almost exactly the same as the percentage from the famous survey there of 1916. They predicted then that disbelief in God would increase as scientific education spread. Hasn't happened though.'

'Shame.'

'But there have been some interesting changes since then. In 1916, it was the biologists who led the disbelieving way. But these days they're believing again – and it's the physicists and astronomers who are the most doubtful. Eighty per cent of them are disbelievers, while it's the mathematicians who are most likely to be on their knees in prayer. Make of it all what you like.'

'I've never met a nice mathematician.'

'And there is, of course, a general awareness that just as 'twinkle twinkle little star' hardly does justice to our current state of knowledge concerning the universe we inhabit, so what they all learnt in Sunday School may not be the last word in the case for Christianity – nice though it was colouring in Joseph's dreamcoat. Religion does develop.'

'Really? But surely the whole point of religion is that it *doesn't*. Doesn't develop. Surely the basic idea of religion is to loiter gamely in the dim, distant, irrelevant but occasionally cosy past, so that people can take a break from reality? I mean, you seem to add a tambourine to the music group once every four hundred years, but apart from that particular error, it's got to be organised nostalgia or broke hasn't it?

Jenny Jewel was not a believer, and I was finding Merrybum an enjoyably easy target.

'Not so. Christianity is developing all the time. The story is the same, but you can tell a story in a thousand different ways, depending on the context. If someone says to me, "Who's Jesus?" my immediate reply is,

"Who's asking?" Belief must risk immersion. Total immersion. It constantly immerses itself in the sea of contemporary assumptions, mixing with the sewage and the salt and, yes, looks worryingly out of its depth sometimes, even to the extent of its head going under, and there's panic on shore and recrimination aplenty. Who let it go out by itself?! It should have stayed on dry land, or at best just paddled! But then there it is again, suddenly vigorous, waving not drowning, and ensuring that the good news of Jesus Christ is not a rock-pool side-show but part of the incoming tide.'

Not on my beach.

*

We were waiting for Archbishop Musselly. Still no sign of Little apparently, but as I didn't know who or what Little was, I wasn't greatly concerned. Just going with the flow.

'She hasn't been seen for twenty-four hours.'

'Who is she?'

'No one really knows.'

'But we do know that her name isn't Little?'

'We don't think it is. She's got called that in her absence, if you see what I mean. I'm not sure, frankly.'

'So no one knows who she is or what her name is?'

'Er, well, someone must know who she is and what her name is. She's somebody's daughter, after all.'

If you are what you eat, then Merrybum must have eaten a lot of tedious nonsense in his time.

'But no one on the permanent staff knows who she is, no. It's been very busy here, of course. Providing for a hundred and fifty scientists and psychologists alongside the regular tide of sightseers and day-trippers. It isn't easy for a community of twenty-three. And she never introduced herself.'

'So how do you know she exists?'

'Brother Baldwin met her wandering in the Garden of Holy Knowledge and asked in his gloomy fashion if she was OK, she said no, and Brother Baldwin then said, so that's all right then, and moved on.'

'Why?'

'It's Brother Baldwin's way.'

'Nice.'

'Only truly happy when someone is deeply aware that they are not OK. He can leave them then. They are facing the darkness, acknowledging the abyss. Good. Excellent. They are on the journey. There's hope. He need no longer concern himself. He can leave, considerably cheered by the encounter.'

I *see*.

'Mind you,' added Merrybum, 'he worries *endlessly* about those who think they're fine …'

I crossed Brother Baldwin off my list of people who

I really *must* get to see before leaving – it wasn't a long one – and asked a question.

'She's definitely not a day-tripper?'

'Oh, no. There have been other sightings. We think.'

'You *think*?'

'Well, if it's the same person, yes. In fact, I'm pretty sure *I* saw her. Pretty girl. She was sitting in the small chapel. Asked me how Van Gogh could paint such hopeful flowers and then shoot himself. It was a question which seemed very important to her. But I wasn't much help. I didn't know he *did* paint flowers.'

'His sunflowers have acquired a little fame along the way.'

'Ah. That must have been what she was referring to. But then I used to be an accountant, you see.'

And then Archbishop Musselly came in.

'Does anybody here know anything about Van Gogh?' he said.

'Funny you should say that,' replied Merrybum.

'I don't see anyone laughing.'

'No. Well, I was just telling Miss Jewel how little we know about, er, Little.'

'Well we're going to need to find out a damn sight more and quickly. Because unless I'm mistaken, I'm holding in my hands a letter she's written.'

'Oh, that's nice,' said Merrybum.

'I think it's a suicide note.'

'Oh, that's terrible.'

'It might *not* be a suicide note.'

'Oh, that's good.'

'But it does look like one.'

'Oh, that would be *awful.*'

'Could you read it to us?' I asked, trying to break the manic-depressive cycle of Merrybum's responses.

'Certainly.'

He fished around in his habit for some glasses.

'She seems to have been doing an art project on Van Gogh.'

His eyes were clearly not as muscular as the rest of him. He was peering hard at the letter.

'She wrote this:

I chose to do a project on Van Gogh because I really enjoy looking at his pictures and I think he was a very talented artist. Van Gogh was born over a hundred years ago. He painted many pictures but sold very few. It was only after Van Gogh's death that he began to be famous.

One of my favourite pictures by Van Gogh is the 'Sunflowers'. It has been sold for many millions of pounds.

During Van Gogh's life he was often very depressed. He spent some of his time in mental asylums. The only friend that Van Gogh had was his brother Theo. Van Gogh died by shooting himself in the breast. The last thing he said to his brother was 'Misery will never end.' His brother died six months later and they are buried next to each other.

Van Gogh used oil paints for his pictures. He applied them quite thickly. A colour that appears in many of his paintings is yellow. He called it the colour of hope. Perhaps he used it often because he didn't have much hope in his own life.

His last painting was called 'Crows over the wheatfields'. Some people say it is a sad picture, because crows are a sign of death. But I think Van Gogh likes the crows, because they have come to take him home.

I often see the crows. They are my friends too. I saw the crows today. Maybe they will take me home.'

'Well?' said Musselly as he placed the letter on his desk, staring at me.

Between one moment and the next, there is sometimes a chasm. Why did I suddenly feel involved? But I was – beyond the call of natural concern. I very much wanted to walk away, of course. I wanted to leave it. Forget it. Over. But the claws had my innards. I felt them hold, grip and twist. An unknown child drifting into the darkness of death, and I couldn't let it happen. I was reaching out. I wanted her back. She didn't belong to the darkness. She belonged to me. I knew her. Knew her well, and I was going to have to go looking. Little was known. And Little needed to come home. The chasm was crossed. The desert jaunt was over. I knew it then. The jaunt had become a journey. Oh, God. What was it I wanted? I didn't know, but whatever I *did* want, I didn't want this. I'd just wanted to make a programme. I'd just wanted to observe and laugh. I'd just wanted to be interested. But not involved …

★

'*Blackpool, it isn't*, take three: In 1856, Horatius Bonar said this: "No one but the photographer can sketch the desert. Only the photographer can portray the millions of minute details that go to make up the bleakness, the wilderness, the awfulness and the dismal loneliness of these earthly wastes." Someone clearly got out of bed the wrong side all those years ago. Mind you, he does have a point. Blackpool, it isn't. But what on earth is it? What on earth *is* St Raphael's doing here? It's the local library for the pharaohs, certainly. But they don't read like they used to, so is it the end of the line for places like this? I mean, what on earth are holy places doing these days to pass the eternal time? Let's go in and find out. Oh and – *mind the burning bush* …'

★

I'd met with Archbishop Musselly the day after my arrival, and we'd got on like a house on fire: there'd been a lot of heat; it had felt like death and I wished it hadn't happened. And all I'd said was something about the burning bush being bloody useful for barbecues, and he just went into one. Maybe I caught him on a bad day, but he was frightening when angry. His was a terrible energy held in. Especially when it wasn't.

'Dark glasses amusingly placed on the statue,' he said to me, pacing up and down in his study. 'That's all it is, isn't it? How wry. How sideways. How quirky. How post-modern. How tedious. Do you think I haven't heard all the jokes about the burning bush? The trouble is, they don't transform. They don't address the soul. They just give it a half-holiday of small-time amusement. They ponce off history. They leach off significance. But in themselves offer nothing. Dark glasses quirkily placed on the statue of history so we can all have a bloody good laugh and reflect on how clever we are, but when the laughing is over the soul is still empty, still looking.'

'And you think Christianity is the answer?! It's not an answer to any of the questions *I'm* asking.'

'Christianity isn't an answer. It's a messenger, gasping with its dying breath the possibility that in the dark and frightening corners of the woodshed at the bottom of the garden, there might just be love.'

And then I remembered what my dad had always told me to say in RE classes at school.

'Of course, paganism pre-dates Christianity.'

'So does farting,' said Archbishop Mussley, 'but that doesn't make me a particularly avid disciple of it.'

The ace in my pack didn't seem to have delivered. He continued to talk, but wearily and looking away from me. Instead, he was focusing on the desert beyond.

'There really isn't time now to play at point-scoring. We've all been invited to the Millennial Ball, you see, but no one's got any clothes to wear, and the bad news is that the three ugly sisters are God: Marx has dismantled the mystery of history; Nietzche has pulled the rug from the certainties of consciousness and Freud has killed off the dream as anything beyond repressed wish fulfilment. So our wardrobe's empty, apart from small-time navel gazing, reassessment and retrospectives, and not a fairy godmother in sight. So by all means laugh at the statue with the shades. But then cry. Cry hard. Because Cinderella's desperate.'

He spun round, and looked me in the eye.

'Now run along, you stupid girl. You don't know how boring I find you. Make your silly little programme. Be amusing. Be a side-show. Miss the point. And then be gone.'

I felt like Judas being sent out into the night. I also

felt intimidated, abused, patronised and very angry. I hated being called 'girl'. I walked out. And then just walked. I walked the cloisters, the outhouses, the bush, and then I walked them again. Turbulent. Churning. Mind racing. My dad had been right. He'd never let me near a church. 'You can make up your own mind. I'm not having any priest getting to you while you're young. If you're up for that nonsense when you're older then that's your lookout. But it would be the end of a very honourable tradition in this family: five generations of atheism.' For my dad and for myself, I carried the tradition on. I began to feel better. I wasn't alone. There was my dad. I could cope with this. We were a team. Five generations. We were a movement. I'd make this programme for my dad and for the family. I'd show them. And I'd show the monastery and the misogynist at the top. We'd have a laugh at their expense. A good laugh. Mine was an honourable tradition. And I would take my place in it.

★

'So you don't really exist.'

'Not officially, no,' said Rowena.

'And you're not really a nun?'

'Not strictly speaking, no, in that I've never actually taken the vows of poverty, chastity and obedience. The poverty I've experienced, I didn't choose; my chastity was along similar lines to those who fast between meals; and my obedience was primarily a struggle to hear the still small voice amidst the clatter of everything else. Whether I heard aright, I don't know.'

'So who are you?'

'Just another survivor limping back from the disaster in search of home.'

'And this is home? Surrounded by men in black dresses and nine hundred skulls in your front porch?'

'You're forgetting the essential absurdity of life.'

'This place is certainly a good reminder. It's a freak show in the sand so far.'

'From Convention to Absurdity. It's the Second Path of Mysticism. The realisation that wherever two or three are gathered together, absurdity is not far away. In family. Politics. Work. Religion. Wherever. Every convention where people choose to pitch their tent – and everyone must pitch their tent somewhere – is cockroach-ridden with absurdity. It is easy, of course, to see the absurdities of others. Harder to see those you've personally swallowed and based your life on. Rather unsettling, too. Of *course* I live in an absurd place. More absurd than you'll ever know. But so do you.'

She was unaware that I'd spent my entire adult life ripping into the absurdities I saw around me. That's what satire was for. And after five generations of fiercely independent and unconventional thinking in my family, my pedigree was anything other than absurd. I think I of all people could be considered convention-free. To the Second Path of Mysticism, I mentally wrote, 'Doesn't apply.'

CHAPTER FOUR

The Feast

HE was a complete prat. A total anorak. He was a scientist. He probably belonged to the Campaign for Real Ale. He didn't wash his hair. And he was sitting next to me. Oh, my God. I mean, why? Why of all the people he might have been sitting next to at 'The Great Feast' did it prove to be *moi*? In the meantime, he was well-away, which was exactly what I would have been if I'd had half a chance.

'And so, of course, after *that*, the whole conversation took a very amusing turn, because *he* thought I'd said "the economy"!'

The anorak was already chuckling, both in remembrance and anticipation.

'But you did,' I said, 'you did say "the economy".'

'No I didn't! That's just the point! I didn't say "the economy" at all!'

He was well nigh helpless with scientific laughter now, but managed to struggle on.

'No, I said "teleonomy", which is a very different kettle of fish, a very different plate of sulphate indeed, as I think you'll agree.'

'I might if I knew what it meant,' I said smilingly, trying so hard to join in the merriment of this social misfit, whose body was crying out for a white coat and close proximity to a Bunsen burner.

'Teleonomy? Well, teleonomy is the belief that creation moves towards a pre-determined end, which is rather different from the economy, which means – well, I don't know what the economy means – I'm a scientist, – but you can see that this central misunderstanding led us into a whole series of comic misunderstandings! It could have been one of your comedy sketches, it really could. Only it was really happening. You would have loved it.'

I'd be the judge of that, thank you very much.

'Were you in a pub at the time by any chance?' I asked.

'Well, we were, as it happens. A hostelry called the Pickled Newt, as I recall.'

'Probably towards the end of the evening, was it?'

'I cannot deny that by this time we had imbibed a fairly large quantity of a mind-altering substance, also known as Fuller's Peculiar!'

'Yes. Well, that doesn't come as a complete surprise. Still, who said scientists can't enjoy themselves?'

'And you don't know the half of it! Or rather, you know something rather less than fifty per cent of it, to the seventh decimal point!'

'I'm sure I don't, but the percentage of it which I *have* heard is maybe enough for the moment.'

'Ah, well you're into probability now!'

'I probably want to leave.'

'Well, when you're up for more, come back and I'll tell you the one about the fusion of the atomic testicles!'

'I can't wait.'

'It is not unamusing, I can assure you!'

'No, you misunderstand. I can't wait to get away from you. You're very dull.'

He laughed conspiratorially, and I slipped into the throng that was 'The Feast'. Scientists. Drink. Psychologists. Drink. Monks. Drink. Music. Food. And lots of drink. All going splendidly. The sense of enquiring hubbub was immense. Some of the greatest minds in the world all gathered together in 'table fellowship' as Merrybum called it, to discuss life, death, the universe and the chances of Scottish football ever getting back on its feet again. No question was too dangerous. Is there a God? What is Time? Had the journey over millions of years from the African savannah to the present information society been a worthwhile one for Homo sapiens? But perhaps the most frequent question, the issue which they most wanted under the microscope, was the size of Richard Dawkin's book royalties.

★

I withdrew into the darkness of one of the side aisles, where snogging couples groping for condoms were surprisingly absent. It wasn't that sort of a party. Instead, away from the cut and thrust of table talk, there was cooler air. And it gave me space in which to be troubled by what lay ahead. Because I was becoming aware of something. I was becoming aware of a strange haunting and an unlikely mission. It was Little who haunted me, called me, tugged at me. And I knew then that I must find her. Alone in that crowd, still amidst the movement, and quiet amidst the noise, I knew that I must find her. It was settled. The crows were over the wheatfield, circling, swooping, squawking and darkening the horizon. And for some unknown reason, they were leaving me with no choice.

Meanwhile, however, there was the feast …

★

'You're referring, of course, to that seminal little tome from Jacques Monod which closes with the wonderful observation, that "man at last knows that he is alone in the unfeeling immensity of the universe, out of which he emerged only by chance." God's finished, I'm afraid, Abbot,' said the physicist.

The table was littered with bottles and ashtrays.

'So you say,' replied Peter.

'Or to put it another way, "there is at bottom, no design in our universe, no purpose, no evil, no good, nothing but pitiless indifference."'

'You should write for the Christmas crackers. They're always on the lookout for merry quips like that.'

'Clarity returns to our world view!'

'Marvellous. I do like clarity. Faith, hope and clarity. Without the faith and hope.'

'Reality reigns!'

'God bless your majesty.'

'And the bleakness is blinding.'

Peter, as in our first encounter, wore ill-fitting jeans and a slightly tight shirt. Only now he was also surrounded by some slightly tight scientists. And lots of talk, not of ill-fitting jeans, but selfish ones. The selfish gene, which is the new us. The gene with no heart. The successful gene which is surviving the evolutionary process until some bigger, nastier, better-equipped gene turns up to take over. It's every gene for him or herself out there, and frankly no one gives a damn. There are successful genes. And extinct genes, and nothing in between. So for the weak gene, the bruised gene, the fragile gene, the crippled gene or the crying gene, the future isn't bright. In fact, the bleakness is blinding. For the gene which isn't completely selfish and utterly ruthless will find no safety net, no hand held out to help, no Good Samaritan – just a Successful Samaritan or an Extinct Samaritan.

'Sausages,' said Peter knowingly.

'No thanks,' said the biologist.

'You're forgetting the sausage. All of you.'

'The sausage?!' said the astronomer who was clearly one of the eighty per cent.

'The sausage, yes. And more particularly, the philosophical undergirdings of the sausage. They seem very important at this point in this debate,' reflected Peter.

'Do they?!' asked a mirthful physicist, who was hugely enjoying the success of his own particular genes even if, according to Monod, it was all ultimately going to end in tears. 'I didn't realise the sausage had any philosophical undergirdings.'

'Then you ought to get out more,' said Peter, 'because the sausage is a potential time bomb out there.'

They were all laughing. They were laughing at this funny ridiculous man, and they were laughing at the porker in their imaginations.

'Certainly, I've never felt that Einstein's theory of general relativity properly took account of the sausage,' continued Peter. 'I mean, obviously his theory pointed in an illuminating fashion to an expanding universe, thus completely destroying the rather cosy, comfortable, crumpets by the fireside know-where-we-stand-with-things Newtonian universe. Time. Space. Material things all now in dangerous relationship. Yes, it did that.'

'It certainly did.'

'But no mention of the sausage. Strange, isn't it? Very strange. Was he scared or something? Was Albert hoping we wouldn't notice? I don't know. Who can say? We merely note it, chronicle its absence. No mention of the sausage in Einstein's general theory of relativity.'

General puzzlement.

'But then, of course, things moved onwards and upwards. Einstein was then, this is now, and the selfish gene is centre stage. The selfish gene has turned up to instant celebrity and acclaim bidding us to further bleak and dismal thoughts. But again, and forgive me if I'm mistaken, I discern no mention of the sausage. The conspiracy goes on. The sausage remains gagged. It's the nettle which no one is grasping. The sausage, I'm afraid, remains the uninvited and unmentioned guest at the party. But personally, I very much like the cut of its jib.'

'What are you talking about?' I ask kindly, because I sense everyone has given up on him.

'It's funny. That's what I'm talking about. The sausage is funny. It's humorous. I don't know why. Is it the shape? Or is it the word itself? Sausage. Mystery. But put a pound of uncooked sausages on the table where some selfish genes are trying to have a serious conversation, and comedy will appear. Jokes. Sniggers. And I wonder why? Why *do* selfish genes find the sausage so amusing? And so endearing? You know, if they are all as selfish and meaningless and pointless and indifferent and bleak and dismal as everyone claims they are. It's as if they can't spend *all* their time being selfish. They need a break from being ruthless. They need a laugh along the way before they return to being pitiless. They're *pretty* selfish genes. But not *that* selfish, and it's the sausage which finds them out. The comedy in the sausage transcends them, takes them out of themselves. It certainly suggests something beyond the cold, closed meaningless universe which is so often projected these days.'

'Don't tell us. God is the cosmic sausage.'

Huge laughter from assorted scientists.

'Well, I'm no theologian, but I do think that the sausage is one of the classic proofs of the existence of God, yes. I'd put it as the First Classic Proof myself. Disappointing that Aquinas never really developed it …'

★

I'd always wanted to be a clown. But I'd only ever managed to be a comic. It wasn't so much that my genes were selfish. They were just scared. So I became a comic instead, and earned a living hiding behind the sharp, the witty, and the acute, safe and in control. And in the meantime, I was blocking the clown, gagging her, throttling her, holding her back. For clowns are silly and I didn't want to be silly. Clowns are open, vulnerable and I didn't dare to be either. Clowns are stupid, ridiculous, foolish. But I was none of those. For what if it all went wrong? What if I was exposed? What if people laughed *at* me instead of with me? What if people rejected me, cut me out? It mattered so much that they didn't. It mattered that people liked me.

And so I remained the comic I didn't want to be. And held back from becoming the clown I did want to be. And I hated myself for it, of course; and probably lost Chris because I had to lay that frustration somewhere and, as my partner, he happened to be handy. Yet I was powerless to change, for I knew of no one to catch me if it all went wrong. It required a trust which I just couldn't muster. I was the selfish gene, certainly. But above all else, I was the scared gene, the fearful gene.

*

'We do appear to have fallen out rather, I grant you. Religion and science. We used to be such friends, didn't we? But now the perception is that we aren't.'

The conversation at Abbot Peter's table continued to flow.

'Science and religion can never be friends, Abbot. Not any longer. Those days are gone.'

'We managed it in the seventeenth century. You brought all that exciting new information. We brought the awe. It was brilliant.'

'That was then. This is now.'

'But they were good days, nonetheless. You were jolly clever even then, of course, brilliantly calculating with even the most rudimentary of instruments the clockwork of the solar system. Remarkable. But in those days, you at least left open the possibility that it was God who set it all ticking, and was somehow there amidst it all. But really, by the nineteenth century, everything had changed, hadn't it? Those terrible long silences between us, I can feel them still, punctuated by furious rows. Things were really very cool indeed, and do you know who I blame?'

'No. Tell me.'

'I blame reductionism. Never liked him.'

'Look, it's too late for all this. Recriminations get us nowhere. The old days are gone, Abbot, and yes, reductionism has been pretty influential in that.'

'Told you so. He comes along with all his big flash

fancy talk about breaking down each problem into questions which can be answered a bit at a time; his brash dismissal of the big view, the whole view, integrating mind body and spirit, brazenly promising only that if we stick with him, one day, *everything* will be explained, including the moment of creation and why things have mass –'

'– That's the future, yes. Accept it.'

'No. Why should we? Basically, reductionism came along and said, "I've got a bigger penis than religion – how about it?" And you said "Yes." Fickle. And misguided. Reductionism leaves everyone an expert in a very small corner. And everyone a moron in the layout of the house.'

'Well, of course we said yes. The relationship with religion was stale. Unhealthy. It wasn't taking us anywhere. In fact, it was holding us back. We've been on holidays with reductionism which you wouldn't have allowed. And we've loved it. It's been a marvellous century, frankly. Quite exhilarating. Our intellectual horizons have exploded like the big bang itself! Relativity and quantum mechanics have taken over from the Newtonianism which spawned them! The sweet mystery of life is found, in the shape of the information theory and the DNA staircase of life! We have raised our eyes to the heavens and found galaxy upon galaxy!

We have tiptoed in wonder on the surface of the moon! We have doubled our life-span, and decimated illness. It is amazing. Miraculous. Awe-inspiring.'

'I do love it when you're awe-full.'

'Oh, yes. We've seen all manner of things. And there are more trips to come. You could say reductionism has taught us everything we know.'

'Granted. But size isn't everything.'

'It's quite a lot.'

'But not everything.'

'The one with the small penis would say that, wouldn't he?'

'Maybe. But that doesn't mean he isn't right. Impure motives don't necessarily mean a complete absence of insight. Many small corners do not a house make. And, you know, I'm just sitting here looking at the way you comb your hair forward.'

'I beg your pardon?'

'The way you comb your hair forward,' shouted Abbot Peter, in an attempt to be heard. 'The way you comb it forward from the centre of your scalp. The way you ask it to travel that long and slightly unnatural journey to your forehead –'

'All right, all right,' replied the scientist, in damage limitation mode.

'No, I quite understand. I understand why. Of course

I do. I'm on your side. You want to disguise the great thinning taking place on your bonce. Absolutely. But do you know what I'm thinking?'

'No.'

'I'm actually thinking, how delightful! Yes. I'm thinking, What a marvellous little vanity in this selfish gene. So human. So endearingly silly. So pathetically dishonest. The hair combed forward. Fooling no one and yet clung to like a life-raft five hundred miles from home. And you know, reductionism will never be able to explain that sort of thing. But religion can, because religion understands the soul, the little aspirations, the strutting pomposities, and the limping hurts.'

'Yes. Well, three bloody cheers for religion but maybe there are rather more pressing matters in the world to be considered,' replied the scientist, casually shifting his hair in a more sideways direction.

'Indeed, there are, but it's so often the details which find us out, isn't it? And the way people comb their hair forward is just one of those details. You wouldn't, for instance, find a dog who forward-combed. It's very human and suggests there's more to this selfish gene than meets the eye.'

Things were getting noisier in the background. Most of it was coming from the psychologists' corner. Peter had to raise his voice to continue, and he continued with the hair, despite the extreme embarrassment of the scientist.

'I know what you're going to say, of course. You'll tell me, no doubt, that what we have here is a basic survival instinct.'

'Pardon?'

'You'll say that male forward-combing is part of the evolutionary process. When the successful gene begins to age, and hair begins to transfer itself from head to back in unsightly fashion, the male of the species must attract the female of the species in new ways in order to propagate. And so he comes up with the idea of combing his hair forward. Brilliant. One of the great evolutionary solutions, ensuring an appearance which is overpoweringly attractive to the female. Mating should almost be instant, and the survival of the species sorted. Phew! But, of course, that isn't so, is it? Oh, dear me, no. Most women fall off their chairs with laughter when approached by a forward-combed male. Have you found that? Have you noticed that women aren't exactly gagging for it from a forward-combed male?'

I was feeling my neck. I was feeling for the wrinkle that I'm sure was developing there. One, maybe two. I could feel them sometimes. Let's face it, my time was running out. Aged thirty-four I'd been told that I had one more year till everything began to droop, sag and wither. I stuck my chin out a little more, and felt the wrinkle ease. Posture. I must remember posture. It was going to be increasingly important from here on. Chin out. Hold head high.

'Forward Combing is, of course, the Third Proof of the existence of God,' said Peter.

Discussion was getting almost impossible. The psychologists were beginning to sing songs standing on tables, that sort of thing.

'With the sausage as the First Proof, yes?' replied the scientist in an amused sort of way, trying to get back to safer territory.

'Yes.'

'So what's the Second?'

'Sorry?'

Someone was singing about the good ship Venus. He had no trousers on. He was very eminent in his field, but probably couldn't have told you what that field was at this particular moment.

'What's the Second Proof of the existence of God?'

'Why? Are your secular defences wilting under my onslaught?'

'No. I'm just hoping that at least one of them will be serious. I hate to see a man make a complete fool of himself.'

'You're too kind.'

And then the table went over. Peter was too slow to catch his beer. It smashed near my feet. The guilty party were a large number of psychologists, holding each other by the waist and forming a large snake-like line, crashing through the table talk with no particularly obvious destination.

'They're fine with clients,' said Peter as he dabbed at his soaking trousers. 'It's just normal relationships they struggle with. So alcohol tends to be very attractive. It's clients or oblivion with them. No middle ground. Tonight, it's oblivion. I wouldn't mind but the psycho-therapist I'm due to meet with tomorrow is the one second from the front with his pants on his head …'

*

I walked with the religious and the scientist under the big night sky. Deep dark velvet, with pin-pricks of incredible brightness. The religious, the scientist and the comic. Sounded like the beginning of a joke. There was once a religious, a scientist and a comic in the desert. But they were all rather tired and didn't really have much to say to each other and, as no genie appeared offering them three wishes or anything simi-lar, that was about as far as the joke got …

It was getting chill, but good to be out of the fug. The party was ebbing to a close. Above us, Mount Sinai was a huge dark shadow. Beyond us, the silence.

The day-trippers had all gone home. They'd all be tucked up now, the adventure of another day over. One day further from birth. One day closer to death, yet content with their deluxe cruise boat on the Nile and why shouldn't they be? They had en suite facilities, they had colour TV, radio and telephone, and individual climate controls in their cabins. They were a short evening stroll from the lounge, the dance floor, the large swimming pool and the bar. The burning bush was safely in the video thank you very much, and frankly £540 for seven nights was proving ever such good value ...

Not all the day-trippers were an evening stroll from the dance floor, of course. Not all had climate controls in their pockets. For some were out there now in their tents. Less en suite, and more on rock, which is preferable only to being on camel. Perhaps even now they were easing off their stout walking shoes, rubbing at aching feet, and seeking warmth in the vast stony spaces around a fire. Yes, they'd be in a circle round the fire with the herdsmen, eating goat stew, reflecting on the day that had been and looking forward to the Valley of the Kings at Thebes tomorrow. Sixty-two royal tombs there. That's a lot of death. The desert was big on death. Take death away from the desert and there really wasn't that much life at all, to be honest.

It was one big cemetery. Life hugs the Nile but death hugs the desert. Sand and death. Sand, rock, death and silence.

I wouldn't have minded being hugged right now. Wouldn't have minded at all. But wandering in this large cemetery in the shadow of the burning bush (retired) with a religious and a scientist, options were limited. I didn't fancy being hugged by either of them. The hug would have to wait.

'You were going to tell us about the Second Proof for the existence of God, before we were interrupted,' ventured the scientist.

'Ah, yes.'

Pause.

'You seem a bit distracted, Abbot.'

'I am.'

'You'd mentioned the sausage and the, er –'

'The hair being combed forward,' I added, seeing that the scientist was struggling with that one.

'Yes,' said Peter. 'I am a little distracted. I was just contemplating my session with my psychotherapist, that's all. And musing upon exactly how I'm going to manage the traditional client/patient relationship. After tonight, you understand. After the song. And the pants. Particularly the pants, I think.'

'He was only having a bit of a laugh. Boys will be

boys!' said the scientist. 'I'm sure we've all put our pants on our head at some point in our lives.'

Numerous examples didn't spring to mind.

'Maybe,' said Peter graciously, 'but it was useful, you see, for me to believe in the myth of personal integration in my healer. Foolish maybe, but useful. I would have preferred it if the myth hadn't been quite so rudely shattered.'

We wandered further from the embers of the Feast Further into the stillness of the night.

'Silence,' said Peter.

'Yes,' I said. 'Nice, isn't it?'

'I mean, The Capacity for Silence. It's the Second Proof for the existence of God. Deep, reflective silence which longs to understand the heart. So distinctively human. So profound. And so beyond. The Capacity of Silence in the human. That completes the trilogy of Proofs. The Sausage, the Silence and the Hair. But to be honest, none of them is helping very much at the moment. Proofs are all very well for people who like the sense of order and manageability which lists bring to existence, but in themselves they in fact prove very little really, unless accompanied by experience. Can anything worthwhile be proved? I don't think so. And now I need to walk alone for a while. So if you'll excuse me –'

'Certainly!' said the scientist with a little too much enthusiasm, which didn't bode well because I sensed his genes wanted to get closer to mine. Peter smiled, and set off. He was tall but slightly stooped, arms folded tight to keep off the cold but head set towards the skies. He was looking up. Perhaps he was looking for help. Well, he must have looked up there once and seen what looked like movement in the heavens. Perhaps he was hoping for a repeat performance tonight. In the meantime, I needed to get away from the scientist who was now inviting me back to his room to play Scrabble. Being a selfish gene, I said no. It was bed time. Today seemed to have disappeared somewhere, although I wasn't exactly sure where. Tomorrow, I really must get down to some serious filming. And then, of course, there was Little. She was out there somewhere tonight. Out there in the wheatfield. I just hoped I could beat the crows ...

CHAPTER FIVE

The Polish Pig

'I don't find apologising easy, but I'm apologising now. I'm sorry. I mistreated you yesterday. I know that.'

'Words are easy,' I said rather easily.

'Not for me they're not. Not words of apology anyway. You're hearing something quite rare.'

I could believe it. Archbishop Musselly spiralling down into a silent depression of self-hate, I could imagine. But saying sorry? To a woman who he had no time for? When his life was disintegrating beneath his feet? No, words weren't always easy. He stood before me, square as ever, with some paper in his hand. He saw me looking at it.

'Not good news. And not doing my blood pressure much good. It's worse than we thought. The salt water is really doing very serious damage to our foundations, and it's a massive operation to deal with it. And very costly.'

'What about Holy Dawn Productions? The answer to the holy man's prayers, aren't they?'

'Maybe.'

'Two million for a few cameras around the place and a millennium morning commentary which will be over and forgotten by lunch. Sounds pretty much like an answer to prayer to me. Not to say a miracle.'

'Maybe.'

'Or does the answer to prayer have to be more spectacular? Do the waves have to part in answer to prayer? Does it only count as an answer to prayer if lightning strikes, crutches are cast aside and at least seven pigs are seen flying by? Couldn't the answer just lie in a good business deal, like it has to for the rest of us?'

'Again, maybe.'

He paced the floor, caged by a problem which he couldn't sort. He was hearing me, just, but inner turbulence was making listening difficult for him. The energy inside him was still only just being contained by his squat body. The day he let slip the dogs of war within might be a day that he regretted. It would be hard to see him turning back, and by then, what damage done?

'If it's OK, I'd like to look for Little,' I said.

'Fine by me.' He seemed pleased by the diversion. 'Yes, we're very stretched at present, with this being the weekend of the Feast. Were you there last night?'

'Yes,' I said with a suitable so-I-know-just-how-bad-it-was-and-how-much-you-must-be-regretting-the-whole-wretched-business inflection.

'Good, eh?'

Wrong again, Jenny.

'Er, yes, very good.'

'I thought it was brilliant. Absolutely brilliant.'

'It went very well.'

He must have been at a different event from the farce I attended.

'Yes, I thought so, too. Good to see them letting their hair down, wasn't it, and just having a wild thrash. You see, they just don't get the opportunity as a rule, these people. They don't get out much.'

This was rich, coming from a monk in the desert.

'They're all so bloody eminent,' he continued, 'that's the trouble. They can't relax. But here, they can. Here, with no one looking on, well, they're free! No one to tell on them the next morning.'

No one to mention the pants.

'Yes, all very healthy,' he concluded.

'Not a *lot* of dialogue across the various disciplines. Wasn't that the basic idea?'

'Action is dialogue. Having a good time in someone's front room is dialogue. They had a good time in our front room. To me, that's dialogue. That's friendship. That's a breaking down of the walls that divide, a refusal to allow the partitions to go up.'

'So there was no trouble later on then?'

'Oh, there was the usual 3 a.m. attempt on Mount Sinai, but we're quite strict on that now. We always make sure there are two or three of our large monks on the gate to stop people leaving. The psychologists are the worst ones. They get maudlin and want to go and repent, and think wouldn't it be marvellous to do it on Sinai. But it's too cold and too dangerous a climb. Hard enough in the chill and sober heat of day, but in their condition? No. The steps towards the summit are terrible.'

'Can't be worse than yours.'

'And what's repentance worth anyway, if it's not remembered in the morning? Alcoholic repentance is, I'm afraid, sentimental shite.'

'I wouldn't know. Not my line of business.'

'You're teetotal?'

'No. I'm happy-with-myself total. I don't repent.'

'Oh, I see. Shame. Still, you're going to find Little for us?'

'I'd like to, yes.'

'Good, good. Very good.'

He was restless. Pacing and restless.

'Have you any idea how long we've been here, Jenny?'

'Ten minutes? Can't be much more. Why – do you have to be somewhere else?'

'No. I mean, this monastery. Do you know how long this monastery has been here? Do you know when it was built?'

'550 AD.'

That's right. 550 AD. So we've been here fourteen centuries. Quite old, eh? About the same age as our most famous work of art, in fact, the icon of Christ, Ruler of the Universe. Seen it?'

My mind drifted back to Fr Lopez' library tour, but I couldn't get much beyond the bewildered Japanese translator, the sweating Strict Baptist from Bournemouth and the scroll of Thucydides being dropped on the floor.

'We saw a lot. Yes, I think I remember it. But to be honest, one icon looks pretty much like another to me. Not being an expert. Or indeed, a believer. Flaky gold paint, haloes various, and gaunt-faced individuals doing odd things with their fingers seems to sum up most of the holy paintings we saw.'

Musselly did his best to control his choking at the inadequacy of my response.

'It was made in Constantinople,' he said, recovering his throat. 'Craftsmen. They used the encaustic method of painting. Molten wax is poured onto the wood. Remarkable durability. Neither the colours nor the message – that Jesus was wholly human and wholly divine – have diminished in the slightest over that time. They've lasted. The icon. This monastery. Lasted fourteen hundred years, seeing off everything which nature and man could throw at them. The gates of hell have never prevailed! Until now. Now, however, the water is seeping amidst our foundations, salt is rotting the granite which holds us, the gates of hell are eager with anticipation and who should turn up as our prospective saviour but the businessman from hell, Mr Delbaba.'

'I sensed you weren't the best of friends.'

'Fourteen centuries of existence. People take that for granted, you know. That somehow it's easy to last a long time if you're religious, but it isn't. Not out here it isn't.'

Not at home either. I was thinking particularly of Cliff Richard and the strains he'd endured.

'You don't last that long in a place like this without a good deal of diplomatic skill, of course. Good relations with Islam have been crucial at times. Hence the minaret.'

'So it *is* a minaret.'

'Oh, yes. Seemed the least we could do after Mohammed himself had affirmed the monks here as the Guardians of the Holy Mountain.'

'He did that?'

'Certainly. The bell for it though was donated by a Russian tsar.'

'Of course.'

There was always a Russian tsar in my experience. In all the best stories, anyway. Russian tsars tended to get up in the morning, buy vast numbers of classic European paintings, and give odd presents to people, like bells to monasteries on Sinai. I'm not sure what they did in the afternoon.

'And then there were the crusaders to be kept sweet as well. After all, they kept crashing through, carving their wretched names everywhere and leaving their coats of arms as calling cards. But we survived. Survived through prayer and, as I say, not a little diplomatic skill. But in all that time, we've never had a saviour like Ted Delbaba. Never.'

'Diplomacy always means compromise.'

'Not that much.'

'This sounds personal.'

'Everything is personal. Anyway, you won't care either way, will you? Whether we stay or go.'

'You seem very sure.'

'Well, will you?'

I wasn't very sure.

*

'It was in late July 1941 when Fr Kolbe took the final steps of his journey into love and darkness.'

Why didn't I want to hear this? But Rowena was going to tell me anyway. She was all heart. We were sitting in her room again. It was at least the one place where I could be sure of a good cup of tea. I'd braved the rats and the skulls to be here, but I sensed there was worse to come. Rowena was quiet, and choosing her words carefully.

'The line of men in the Auschwitz concentration camp knew what was coming. When an individual escaped, then the punishment lay with those who remained.'

Typical. And just like our maths teacher at school. Kept us all in when it was just the boys fooling around. It had always struck me as deeply unfair even then, but my dad had never written to complain. There's unfair, however, and there's unfair. And then there's Auschwitz.

'Random selection for the Starvation bunker,' she continued. 'That was the punishment for those who remained. The individuals would be chosen from the line, stripped, herded into the cell, door closed, and left to rot, left to die by disintegration. Starved and dehydrated, the body becomes no body. Fr Kolbe, though was one of the lucky ones on that particular morning. He wasn't chosen.'

'He *wasn't* chosen?'

'No — not this time. They passed him by. The hand never reached out for his shoulder. He was safe. Cause for celebration. Instead, it was people like Franciszec Gajownickek who felt the hand and knew the worst.'

'Sickos.'

'But Franciszec can't bear it, can he? Could you? And he shouts out, he screams, "My poor wife and children!" He was concerned about them. What would they do without him? How would they cope? Anyway, Fr Kolbe hears his cry and he has a decision to make. And he makes it. He steps forward. He's a Polish priest. Sunken eyes, sunken cheeks, round glasses in wire frames. He steps forward and the guard is angry:

'"What does the Polish pig want? Who are you?"

'"I am a Catholic priest. I want to die for that man. After all, I am old. He is young. He has a wife and children."

'Well, you might think the Nazis would have told him to shut up. The more suffering the better. Wife and children as well? Excellent. We move from hell to sheer hell. But no, because the request by this older priest rather tickled their utilitarian approach to life. Old was useless. Let's kill old. Young can die later when they've served their purpose. When they too are old. So the transaction was done, Kolbe replaced Franciszec and he

77

joined the others being led to Cell 18. It was their final journey. The door was closed, and there, naked on the cement floor they died over the next two weeks. They sang psalms while they could. They said the Mass. They carried on until their bodies could carry on no longer.'

Carry-on up the bunker.

'Kolbe was the last to die, so he died alone. Well, someone had to. He was given an injection of phenol, in fact, to hurry the process because by that time they wanted to clear the cell. They were very tidy and organised like that. An orderly was given the job of emptying the place of the bodies. There was a remarkable sense of holiness in the place. "Sometimes I had the impression I was in church," he said.'

'And that story is meant to encourage me?' I asked.

'The trouble with your little TV programme is that you spend all your time observing.'

'Of course.'

'As you say, of course. Very important. Observation is crucial. But mere observation isn't enough, for it means you don't *relate* to us. And if you don't relate to us, you can't love us. And if you can't love us, then you can't know us. Because knowledge only travels whilst accompanied by love. It can't travel alone. From Separation to Communion. It's the Third Mystical Path. It's there in the story of Fr Kolbe. He could have stayed separate.

78

He could have stayed where he was in the line and shouted an angry and defiant "Good luck!" as they were taken away. Maybe even, "I'll pray for you!" Instead, though, he chose Communion. He could be there for the condemned, because he chose to relate to them.'

'That's what priests are for.'

'It's what we're all for. In you though, I sense only Separation. There is a Separation in you which needs healing; a Separation which needs a Communion to come home to. Is it Little who calls you? Calls you into Communion? Maybe. But I sense in you other calls, other Communions. I sense that you, like Kolbe, face a journey into love and darkness. From Separation to Communion. Could be important, my dear. More tea?'

CHAPTER SIX

The Stunted Plant

VINCENT Van Gogh was born on March 30th 1853, exactly one year after the birth of Vincent Van Gogh. The second Vincent Van Gogh went on to become the famous artist. The first Vincent Van Gogh, his elder brother, was still-born. And the rest, as they say, is history. Which isn't necessarily the same as saying the rest is very dull. Just imagine if the rest were geometry for instance ...

Thankfully, however, it wasn't. It was history. And I had plenty of time to reflect on history. Lots of it. Centuries worth. For we were only half an hour into the three-hour Morning Office. It was 4.30 a.m. and it was cold in the chapel amidst the intoning of the psalms and the other incomprehensible religious activity the bearded men had all dragged themselves out of bed for. *They* all knew what was going on. That was the main thing. The fact that any visitor felt a complete spare part wasn't their problem apparently. If it had worked in the eleventh century there was no reason to suggest that it shouldn't be a rip-roaring success in the twentieth.

There was a little heat amidst the chill from a bank of candles to my right. They could be my salvation. I edged nearer. And sat. Medieval comfort, medieval entertainment. And the hours stretched out before me. 4.32 a.m. Yes, I had plenty of time for history. The Hundred Years War, for instance, between the French and the English suddenly seemed a very brief skirmish indeed ...

I knew what they said, of course. How could it be otherwise really? How could Van Gogh's mother have loved him? No, I mean, I could see it was quite impossible. After the tragedy of a still-born child, the mother just cannot, for love or money, attach herself to the living child – so strong and deep is the desire to keep the dead child alive in fantasy. It's a terrible force with terrible consequences, for it makes a crime of love and care; it makes a firm attachment to the living child an active abandonment of the child who has died. And how could a loving mother countenance that? Dead *and* unloved? The grave is a cold enough place without such additional savage exclusion from the family circle. So the mother loves the dead. And holds back from the living. Of course. The trouble is, the living need loving, too. Young ginger-haired Vincent needed loving ...

I had done my research. I had gone to seek out Merrybum to discover if there was a library on the premises. He'd asked me if I was pulling his leg, for hadn't I visited their magnificent library only two days previously? Had they a library? Was the Nile long and wet?! They had one of the finest libraries in Christendom! I explained that it *was* one of the finest libraries in Christendom if you wanted books that were a million years old, but that one or two things had been written since the flood, and might a selection of those exist anywhere on site? Books which normal people read, I'd added, in the face of his bewilderment.

As it turned out, there was a little collection of post-ark books in the annex where the retreatants lived, and amongst them, a book on Vincent Van Gogh. I came to him knowing nothing other than that he cut off his ear and painted sunflowers. I'd never really liked his paintings. By the time I put the book down, however, something had changed. By the time I'd read his story, scribbled notes and sighed recognition, things were different. I felt like I'd walked a huge bridge across a massive river, and found myself in a new land. This life was for some reason very important to me. Here was a family I understood. It all resonated. I kept having to put the book down, and go for short walks to digest things. I wasn't always sure what I was recognising, but I was recognising something. The social misfit who was Vincent Van Gogh had entered my life. And so had his mother and father and brothers. I'd met them, been introduced and somehow they mattered. I still didn't like his paintings much.

Vincent was the unhappy outsider, the straggly, deformed and stunted plant exposed to a frosty wind by Mother Nature when a seedling and thereafter never quite able to root and grow like the others. Vincent was a boy who was ignored and rejected by a grieving mother whose love and affection inevitably lay with his dead brother. His dead brother Vincent. His dead brother Vincent who he could never match. His dead brother Vincent whose grave was just round the corner from the family home in Zundert, often visited by them, and passed weekly as they went to church. Nice. His dead brother Vincent who he could never match, but who he could perhaps join. In heaven. Vincent Van Gogh – a stranger on earth, with a particular fondness for cemeteries, painting his way towards the trigger and the final reconciliation. The final reconciliation with Vincent. Then he would be equal. Then he would be loved. Because that was one thing he'd learnt – you're only really loved if you're dead …

And I, of course, wasn't thinking of Vincent. I was thinking of Sian. The child who I'd lost nearly fourteen years ago, and who I'd tried so hard to forget because I was told I was young and that time was a great healer. Sian. Still-born. Still. Born, but not born. Dead. Still, plenty of time, though, as the doctor pointed out. Plenty of time for me to have others. Nothing physically wrong with me that they could discern. Just one of those things. Time. That's all I needed. Time to pick myself up, brush myself down and get up and get on with life. It's the best healer of all, time. So mourn, certainly – and then live.

But there's a thin line between healing and hardening; and a thin line between mourning and maiming. I hadn't been healed. I'd been hardened. Hardened to people and to the world around me. And instead of mourning, I'd maimed. Maimed those who didn't understand because *I* didn't understand. Didn't understand why I was picked out for the dead child. Ms Jewel? You appear to be down for the still-born child. If you could just come over here and sign the necessary documentation, then we needn't detain you further.

I would have been a good mother. Unlike so many. So many mothers were hopeless. I saw them in Tescos,

I heard about them on the news. Mothers who couldn't care. Mothers who wouldn't care. But it never seemed a problem for them to have children. They were given plenty. Another child? Certainly, Madam. Here we are, a bouncing baby boy. Now off you go and neglect him like you neglect all your others. Madam would prefer a girl? How very discerning. Just hold on, I'll see if we have one in your size. Ah yes, here we are! And a little cracker, if you don't mind my saying so. She's yours now to screw up completely ...

I would have been a good mother. I think I would. I wanted to be a mother. I didn't really want anything else at that time. Whisper it quietly in the Halls of Alternative Comedy, but I never even wanted a career. I wanted to be a mum. But I wasn't allowed to be. And I had to do something with my grief and anger. It was all very simple, on reflection. The grief I denied, whilst the anger seeped at the foundations of love and trust – and brought the whole lot down.

The frost within Anna Van Gogh: the frost which could never give the germinating Vincent the cooing, nourishing, warming, cuddling climate he craved – I knew it. I knew that frost. I carried it. I lived it. I lived from it. Perhaps if I could get back to Sian, I could get back to Chris and what happened there. Everything was so confused. I was here to make a programme, not a pilgrimage. And yet here I was at 5 a.m. in a strange chapel on a large mountain in a big desert, thinking and thinking and thinking, and not knowing what to do, but knowing I must do something, because everything inside me was aching and crying, in a frustrated and tearless sort of way.

'I think I know where Little might be,' said Merrybum.

I was startled. Startled by the voice from the blue. Or gold. It was mainly gold in the chapel. And startled that it came from Merrybum, who not half an hour ago was sitting in the choir stalls intoning a lot.

'What are you doing here?' I asked.

'What are *you* doing here?' he replied.

Fair question and I didn't know the answer.

'But I suddenly remembered,' continued Merrybum. 'When I met Little, she mentioned the Tomb. It's on the tour for those who are particularly keen, but many miss it off. There's nothing there anyway. It's just a cave of some sort. I don't think it ever really was a tomb.'

'But you've been inside it, this tomb?'

'You must be joking. An adult couldn't get in. Too narrow.'

'But a child?'

'Maybe.'

Maybe? Brilliant. Whatever else they'd been busy

with at St Raphael's over the last fourteen hundred years, it certainly wasn't Health and Safety inspections. What with the stairs and now the Tomb. Their time would come, though. The time would come when the fifth and most terrifying Horseman of the Apocalypse, Health and Safety, would visit the desert. Oh yes. Health and Safety would reach the desert. And then, the desert would know it; then St Raphael's would squeal like a piglet facing the knife. When *they* came, let the reader understand, then the combined threat of Islam, crusaders, burning sun, cracking cold and disintegrating foundations would be as *nothing*. And then it would come to pass that they would dream of the good old days when they were just raped and pillaged. Enter, from the local council offices, the Irritating Man – the irritating man with his book of regulations, tut-tut-tutting his way round the monastery, noting this, jotting down that, and gazing with longing at sub-section 14 paragraph 41, which it was more than his job was worth to ignore. And, oh dear, oh dear, oh dear – what have we here, eh? I don't think we can be countenancing *that*. And just for starters he'd put a bloody great Fire Exit sign in front of Christ, Ruler of the Universe. The universe maybe, Christ. But not here. Here, H & S rule. Here, it is the Irritating Man that you bow to. *Believe.*

'She just said she'd read about the Tomb and wanted to see where it was,' continued Merrybum. 'I said it was dangerous and that she mustn't go there alone, and under no circumstances go inside, and she said no, she wouldn't. She understood, I think.'

'You think? But you're not sure.'

'Who knows what a child understands?'

'Not you, apparently. Still, it's only a death-trap. What harm can it do?'

Irony, I believe.

'And it was then she started talking about Van Gogh.'

'And did that worry you?'

'Like I said, I didn't really know anything about him. Look, I can't stay. I must get back to my place. I'm a novice. A man under authority and all that. My guess is that she's nowhere near the Tomb, that she's probably headed for the top of Sinai. Or maybe taken the coach back to the village.'

'Fine. But just tell me where it is, this Tomb.'

'You go past the bush to that bit of wasteland beyond, where the bins are. There's an incinerator, too, for the monastery rubbish.'

'Nice.'

'Yes, just follow your nose. It stinks. And it's up behind there. You'll find it.'

Those were not encouraging words. I'd last heard

them from the day-tripper about the toilet. 'You'll find it.' But I never did. I'd found everything but. I'd found rats, skulls and a nun who wasn't a nun and didn't really exist anyway. But toilets? No. They were out there *somewhere* I suppose. Somewhere over the rainbow. But they hadn't been there for me. Like God, most famous for their absence.

I got up to leave. I was angry. I found myself half-bowing to the altar, which angered me more. I think I was still trying to please someone somewhere in my past. God knows who and God knows why. So I carried on bending and fiddled with my shoes, as a small act of defiance. Bowing? Me? You're having a laugh. I'm doing my shoes up, stupid. I then walked quickly down the centre aisle. I'd almost reached the main door, when she stepped out from the darkness, and placed a piece of paper in my hand.

'It's number four,' said Rowena.

'What is?' I said testily, because I really didn't want to see her right now. For someone who had been my saviour and a sister in arms, things had taken a turn for the worse. She wasn't being what I wanted.

'It's the Fourth Path of Mysticism.'

'I think you're mistaking me for someone who's interested.'

'It's not about being interested. It's about being saved.'

Sanctimonious garbage.

'Well, who here is saving Little?' I asked.

There. The true voice of prophecy, cutting ruthlessly through all the religious crap.

'*You*,' said Rowena quietly but firmly.

'Precisely,' I said. 'No one else seems to care.'

'On the contrary, we all care. But you volunteered. You said to the Archbishop that it was something you wanted to do. He sensed it was important to you, and said yes. You're doing it for your own reasons. So don't let it become some vehicle of self-righteousness for you, or a means by which you judge and dismiss others. Otherwise it really will be a very sad affair.'

'Yes, well, who knows? I'm going to have a wander round now anyway. Cheery Arse thinks she's probably half way up Sinai or returned to the village. We'll see.'

I didn't want to tell her I was going to the Tomb. It was becoming an increasingly private affair for me.

'So you won't lose it?' she asked.

'What?'

'Number four. Number four of the mystical paths. The paths which prepare you for an encounter with God. They can't *give* you that encounter, of course. But they can prepare the way. It's a particular favourite of mine, number four.'

I'd tried to dislike her and failed, failed miserably,

which was a great disappointment. She really believed all this. I smiled.

'I won't lose it. I'm putting it in my pocket now.'

Fortunately, I was wearing clean knickers this morning, so that if I ended up in the casualty department of Cairo Central Hospital there'd be no embarrassment there. But I was slightly concerned about slipping an unknown piece of paper in my pocket which would probably mark me out as a Christian nutcase to any hospital orderly who kindly sorted through my personal effects. I'd ditch it later. Five generations on atheism breeds strong traditions and a clear eye for preventative measures in matters pertaining to organised religion.

'So you won't tell me what you want from all this? Why Little holds this fascination for you?'

She was following me out.

'No, I won't,' I said, 'but I have my reasons. Let's leave it at that.'

'We'll leave it anywhere you like. It's your life. Good luck. And don't let us girls down!'

She winked in solidarity. She smiled. We hugged. She smelt musty. She disappeared back inside. The intoning continued. And I left, stepping out into the desert morning. A new day. The first day, in fact, of the rest of my life. The poster shop cliché was true. Next I'd be tittering at the amusing observation that you don't have to be mad to work here – but it helps! I must be getting middle-aged. I felt the skin on my neck. I was very conscious of the wrinkling sun. Seemed OK, but I dropped my shoulders and held my head up just in case. Posture. Alexander technique. Puppet on a string and all that. Not that anyone was watching. They were too busy arguing. And it was getting nasty.

CHAPTER SEVEN

Kept in the Dark

'No, I don't accept this, guv'nor. Not at all, no. You are way out of order. Way out of order. After all, how long have I been doing business here?' said Ted.

'That's not the point,' said Musselly. 'You made a promise.'

'I must have been out of my mind, frankly.'

'Your words.'

'So I promised. But anyone can make a mistake. Am I not allowed to make a mistake now? The Church doesn't allow mistakes. Is that it?'

'The contract was pretty clear.'

'Who needs a contract where there's trust? We never needed contacts in the old days.'

'The contract was very clear. And you signed it.'

'And that's it, is it? It's all about money and contracts!

The Church is shit. This monastery is shit. I tell everyone. They all agree. They can't believe it. All you want
is money. All you want is your thirty pieces of silver.'

'You've been landing your helicopter on our site for
four years now, bringing visitors here. How much have
you earned from those trips?'

'I earn *nothing*. Nothing. Well, I make a bit. I survive.
But that's all. I can't afford what you're asking. That's
silly money. I never paid before. Not with the last
abbot. Decent man the last abbot. Christian gentleman,
him.'

'And senile. So a good man for you to do business
with. You screw him deliberately and calculatingly for
every penny you can, and he says thank you very much,
Mr Delbaba, and God bless you, my child. You didn't
have to sign.'

'Look, I don't see everything which crosses my desk.
I'm a busy man. So I signed a contract! I can't believe
this. No one can believe this. I employ fourteen people.
They can't believe this. They think you're shit. I won't
be landing again.'

'That's true, you won't be landing again, but that
isn't the point. Whether you land here again is irrelevant. What we're trying to do here is face the past. You
have landed here for four years. And you've never paid,
even though you agreed to. Can't you see that?'

'I can see that the Church is shit. That's what I can see ...'

It hadn't been hard to listen in. They were standing near one of the side chapels. But I'd had enough. I was suddenly aware that I had a great backdrop for the opening shot of the programme. The stillness. The early morning intoning in the background. Yes, if I set up just outside the chapel, I could get both. And I could explain about Little. Make it all a bit quirky, a bit wry, a bit sound-bitey. I wouldn't tell the truth obviously. This was TV.

I collected the gear from my cell, set it up despite my cold fingers, and began to shoot.

'*Blackpool, it isn't*, take four: I don't know what gets you out of bed in the morning. But I doubt it's this!' (Amusing roll of eyes, as I indicate chapel behind me. A man is singing some prayers solo, sounding dire and in great pain.) 'They're at prayer here at St Raphael's. And it's awful! That's right. Full of awe. Well, they're full of something anyway. It's 6.15 a.m. and they've been at the Morning Office since 4 a.m. Or is it the Moaning Office? I sometimes wonder. And if you want to know what a *good* day at the Office is, dear, it's about fifty-eight psalms, chanted. So a *bad* day doesn't bear thinking about. Still, there's always the 'Office Party' to look forward to at Christmas. It's the same, only with more psalms and a very large Advent candle. They make their own fun here, I can tell you.

'So Blackpool, it isn't. But what is it? Well at the moment, St Raphael's is a missing persons bureau. Yes. I've walked in to a real Enid Blyton adventure here, and I'm jolly golly-gosh excited, and feel like singing a song all about it, just like Noddy does. But I can't compete with them.' (Another wry back glance at chapel and terrible intoning.) 'So I'm going straight to where the missing person was last seen. Very near a rather famous, but sadly retired, burning bush. See you there.' CUT.

I carried the equipment round the corner towards the bush. It was still very quiet. I was climbing slightly, revealing down below and beyond the walls a huge beyond of rocky sparse expanse. The only human imprint on all this, a winding road disappearing into middle distance. The day-trippers, the daily deliveries of food, the new retreatants, the next conference – they'd all soon be travelling along it. The bedouins would watch them come and watch them go. Gone were the days when the monastery was three days' travel on the back of a camel. There was car park at the foot of Mount Sinai now. And discarded pizza boxes where Moses had once passed round the famous tablets of stone.

But you couldn't do much with the mountains above. No car park there. Their profound inhospitality was overwhelming. There were steps to the summit of Sinai. But they were designed for mountain goats, not humans. This was poor planning, because the mountain goats couldn't really give a toss about Sinai, while the humans were just aching to get up there. Literally.

I'd reached the bush. The burning bush. I put the equipment down. And looked at it. It was large. Taller than me. But then I was small. Maybe Moses was small. You'd certainly feel small if this thing was alight and there was a deep voice coming out of it. Shoes off sooner than look at you, lots of bowing, scraping and imploring, and basically saying yes to anything asked of you. Egypt? Fine. Of course I'll go to Egypt. Major Escape Plan to get the Israelites out? Why not? All of them, you say? Ambitious, but a cracking idea, nonetheless. First rate. Just wondering if I'm exactly what you're looking for, of course. Not hugely experienced in that department. Not saying I can't or won't. But, er, just a herdsman, me. Nothing special. And then there's that man two valleys along who looks very like me. Complete spit in fact. We're often mistaken, yes! And he's ever so good with his hands and probably full of practical escape plans for large numbers of people. I can well see him rising to the occasion splendidly. And a marvellous wife. Two for the price of one there, if you play your cards right. No, Lord? No. I see. I'm getting the picture. It isn't him you're after. It's me. Marvellous. I'm the one. The one that you want. Almost feel a song breaking out. Egypt it is then. Fine! I'll get packing right away. Smashing, super, lovely.

And off Moses jolly well went. Not these days, though. Things didn't work like that now. Bushes didn't talk. They hadn't done since science began to pension off religious stories as surplus to requirements. A painful downsizing of the world for some, but very necessary. You just didn't say yes to bushes these days, God didn't say much these days. Mind you, mine was a sort of yes. It wasn't a Moses yes. Not a religious yes. It was a secular yes. But it was a yes all the same. In that I could have said no. But I'd said yes. Said yes to Little. That's why I was standing here now. I had my reasons. I wasn't absolutely clear about what they were, but I knew a little bit more now than I knew two days ago. I knew, for instance, it wasn't just about Little. There was Sian. There was Chris. There was the inner frost. Was there God? …

I was looking at the bush and I was being asked a question. Are you serious? The bush was asking me if I was serious. Obviously it wasn't the bush talking. But I experienced the question whilst standing next to it.

Serious, Jenny? Because beyond the bush was the bit of wasteland Merrybum had spoke of. And beyond the waste ground was the Tomb. And beyond that – well, we'd see. Probably nothing, actually. Probably all turn out to be a complete waste of time. Little was probably sitting having breakfast now with all the other residents. I could turn back. Have a quick look behind the incinerator and go back and say, 'No luck', and they'd all say, 'Well thanks for trying, you're a brick', and everything would be fine.

But I knew I wasn't going to do that. Not this time. Because it wouldn't be fine. I wandered across the Wasteland. Nothing too dramatic. I was just looking, investigating, that sort of thing. Let's keep it relaxed. Nothing was settled. Casual interest concerning the vague possibility of the entrance to the Tomb. And there it was. Suddenly, the entrance. I'd heard it spoken of. Circled around it in my imagination. And now here it was. The Narrow Door. Literally. A little plaque, scuffed, old and overgrown with various desert weeds, sat next to it saying, 'Struggle to enter by the Narrow Door.'

The door wasn't a door, but a crack in the rock. I could see why Merrybum had never been inside. He couldn't fit. But I could. Because I was small. I could squeeze in, have a quick poke around and then squeeze out again. I'd been planning on taking the camera but there was no way that was possible. The struggle to enter the Narrow Door ruled out all baggage. I'd have to leave it by the bush. Anyway, I wouldn't be there long. I'd be out again in a minute.

I looked back at my camera. It was fifty yards away. I could go back to it. But then again I couldn't. The casual stroll across the waste ground had been a significant part of the journey. There was no going back. Just a going inside. I was here and this was it. This is what it had all been leading up to. And I didn't feel at all like Noddy on a jolly exciting golly-gosh adventure with a large tea, courtesy of Mrs Tubby Bear, waiting for me at the other end. In fact, I felt slightly ill. And tired. And where was Big Ears when you needed him?

'Don't worry about what you find,' he said.

It wasn't Big Ears. It was Tight Shirt. It was Abbot Peter. And I was surprised.

'What are you doing here?'

'The clue, my dear Watson, lies in the sack of rubbish in my hand and my close proximity to the bins.'

I have to say I was glad to see him.

'You'll have to go in, I'm afraid. I can see that. It's your calling. But don't worry about what you find. It's quite safe.'

It was good to hear an authoritative and encouraging

word about the Tomb. It was safe, apparently.

'What is it that you want, anyway?' he asked.

'I just want to look.'

I tried to sound as casual as possible.

'Well, looking is very frightening. But not as danger-ous as not looking. So, as I say, don't worry about what you find. You're quite safe. That's the important thing. I've been looking myself recently. Indeed, I was sent here to look. Look inside myself. Not inside the Tomb, of course. I'd never fit.'

'Couldn't be more of a squeeze than your shirt.'

'Yes. Well, I have to say the clothes aren't mine. Mine aren't as nice as this. They were left by day-trippers various, and the monastery kindly keeps them for people like myself who turn up without a huge amount to wear.'

'So why did you turn up at all?'

'Trouble at my own monastery. I was sent on com-passionate leave.'

'What sort of trouble?'

'Well, I didn't have my hand in the till. Big clue.'

'So it was sex?'

'Ah. You know the Church better than I thought.'

'I know a clergyman. He buried my mother. He always said bishops could get away with anything and everything. As long as it wasn't money or sex.'

'The first two Commandments, indeed. But actually, I haven't been so happy for years. I see my psychotherapist. We chat about this and that. I do some spiritual reading. And I wander around meeting people, marvelling at their stories. I pray. I listen. Should have done it years ago. It's really very good being loved. Takes all the fear out of looking.'

'Am I loved?'

'Ah. That would be telling.'

'I thought telling was in your job description.'

'No. I'm not very good at telling. No one told me, you see. And for that I am truly grateful. It meant I could have the *experience* of love instead of words *about* it. You may be loved. Who knows? Do you feel loved?'

'No.'

'Then that's hard. Very hard. Maybe in the short term all you can do is stay within listening distance of God's silence. But, as I say, don't worry about what you find. Because it can't hurt you.'

'How can you be so sure?'

'Look, metaphysical discussions about the nature of reality are for inebriate students in provincial universities the world over after one o'clock in the morning has struck. Me? I'm just here to dump my rubbish. And then I'm having coffee with a scientist who thinks I'm a complete tosspot although, strangely enough, I still think we could be friends. Yes, definitely. Agree to disagree but disagree to part, that's what I say. I'll look after the camera, by the way.'

'Thanks.'

'Yes, I know just the place for it. Just the place. And don't worry. There may be something in the woodshed at the bottom of the garden. But it can't hurt you. Because in the darkest corner of the woodshed is love. Imagine it.'

With a big heave, he threw the bag of rubbish into one of the skips. There was a loud tear as the shirt and buttons gave up the struggle, ripped hopelessly apart by a body too large.

'Oh dear. That's the trouble with most of the tourists here being Japanese.'

'I did wonder about your almost slavish commitment to Mitsubishi over the part few days.'

'Yes. Marvellous ball-handlers in the three-quarter line, of course. Brilliant. But while their largest forward is five foot four inches tall, they'll never really be a force in world rugby, will they?'

I hadn't a clue what he was talking about.

'Or indeed a very helpful supplier of shirts for me. Whatever happened to forgetful fat Americans at St Raphael's? Go well, Jenny.'

He turned towards the main buildings. I watched

him amble round the corner. I liked him. Even if he was a pervert. Who knows anyway? I looked up at the big sky. I took a last look around. I breathed in deep the air that was beginning to warm and turned towards the opening in the rock. I placed my hands against the stone. And began gently to work my body through the hole. The Narrow Door.

★

There's dark and there's dark. And then there's dark. There's city dark which is slightly dark sometimes if you're a bit of a distance from the neon. And there's country dark, which is much darker because there's no neon for five miles. Just cow dung. And then there's desert dark, which is the darkest by far because this is the desert, frankly, and everything has to be extreme, otherwise it wouldn't be the desert. And so if you want dark you step inside a desert cave, and it's pitch. And it's black. And you can't see, and you won't see. Ever. And I'd dropped my torch and I couldn't find it. And this was ridiculous because I needed it. The sand was cool in my fingers as I groped around.

'Little?' I said quietly, before realising that this wouldn't be a name Little knew. 'Er, is there anyone here? I've come to help.'

Silence. Certainly I didn't sense anyone. But then I still didn't know what I was inside exactly. It could be an enormous cavern. It could be a tiny cave. If only I could find my torch. This was ridiculous. And then I did. Something hard and plastic. But not a torch. I picked it up, felt it, held it, ran my fingers along the contours and very quickly realised I was holding a hair clip. So someone had been here or was here. And probably a girl. My heart beat as my fingers searched on for the torch. One tramp to another: 'Got a light, Mac?' 'No, but I've got a dark brown overcoat.' Joke last used at the Bound and Gagged Club, Saturday night, Tufnell Park Tavern. It was important to keep a record.

And then there it was, which was a big relief, I had my torch back, only it didn't work, which wasn't a big relief. My torch didn't work. The one time in my life when I had really needed it, and it didn't work. I banged it, shook it. No good. I'd accepted the loss of my camera with fairly good grace. But the loss of my torch. This was getting stupid. Did I feel loved? No. Not at all. Not in the least. I was crying out for a break but not this sort. I began to feel around the walls to get some idea of size. It appeared that it was small. I could reach the ceiling easily, and four large paces took me from one side to the other. The rock inside was dry. I began to sense it was some kind of lobby or porch to something further within. So this wasn't the Tomb itself, maybe? Had Little gone further inside? But how?

And then the awful discovery. The hole. At ground level at the back of the cave was a tunnel in the rock. About two foot high. A tunnel into a fourth level of darkness, when I'd already failed on level three. I could, of course, turn back. Just outside was the light and my camera. But Little wasn't here and I'd come to find Little. It would mean crawling on my knees into a terrible unknown. And it was the hardest decision of my life, because claustrophobia was a big one for me, always had been. And I wouldn't have gone, but for the noise. I heard something. So faint. But it was something. Something ahead. Something through the tunnel. Something which called me to a journey of love and darkness ...

'Is there anyone there?' I asked quietly. I was frightened of the dark. 'Is there anybody there?' Slightly louder.

Anyone would do. Little. Chris. Sian. The Anorak even. That's how desperate I was. No reply. I began to crawl. I was mad. But I was compelled. I got down on my knees, glad to be wearing jeans, and began to crawl through the hole.

CHAPTER EIGHT

On Your Knees

Pᴀᴅᴅʏ is walking down the street in Belfast. Suddenly he feels a gun at his head, and a voice says, 'Are you Protestant or Catholic?' Paddy has to think quickly. 'I'm Jewish,' he says. 'Well, well, well,' says the voice behind him, 'if I'm not the luckiest Arab in all of Ireland ...'

A confession. I'm on my knees anyway, so it seems like a good time. I hadn't actually done live stand-up comedy for two years and the reason wasn't an absence of bookings. My agent had me lined up for a national tour of decently sized venues. But I couldn't do it. No way. Quite simply, I'd lost my bottle. And you need bottle to go out there, stand-up and deliver. You need bottle to place your life in their hands. Because there's no safety net. You live or you die. They want you or they don't want you. And if they don't want you, that's hard. You can hate them, but it's still hard. You can rationalise till daybreak but it's still hard.

So you've got to be a fundamentalist for something, even if it's only the power of laughter. To stand up, you've got to believe. But I wasn't a fundamentalist for anything any more. Not a believer in anything any more. I just didn't know. I didn't feel I had anything to say. I had jokes to crack and observations to make, but they weren't adding up to anything. Musselly was right. I was a side-show, an irrelevance. Exist to resist. But resist what? I wasn't part of the struggle. I wasn't part of the solution. Which meant I was part of the problem.

Comedy is a crusade ultimately. It's a revolution. It's an amusing rudeness which is designed to mock, shake and ultimately pull down pretentious or evil structures. It's a bomb to derail bigotry. All that stuff. As I say, it's a crusade. That's how I understood it anyway. But you have to believe in something to volunteer for a crusade. And you have to feel as you plant the bomb by the rail track and watch the explosion and twisting metal and listen to the screams and whimpers – you have to feel there's a point. You have to feel right. And you have to feel that there is a difference to be made. That beyond this there is something better; beyond the destruction, some construction. I'd lost that. I'd lost that belief, I'd lost that feeling. I'd lost hope. No confidence, no hope, no crusade, no stand-up. Just sit down …

I knew when it happened. It was after a gig at the Apollo in Birmingham. There was a news story around at the time about the struggle to have built a monument of remembrance to the gays who died under the Nazis. Fifty thousand of them. I'd been doing my pieces on stage. Here was surely a moral crusade and in the Holocaust it seemed to me I had a powerful tool of remembrance. I used the Arab in Ireland joke. I used plenty of others. Rasping stuff against all forms of xenophobia.

Afterwards, a quietly spoken Afro-haired student with brainy glasses came up to me and simply said, 'You do know that you're wasting your time?'

Thanks.

We'd got talking, you see. He said he liked the show, and I said cheers, and prepared to move on. Adulation's nice but I had a bus to catch, a world to change and 'Stars in their Eyes' recorded on the video. Then he went and ruined it all. The evening. Everything. He said I was wasting my time; said that the Holocaust, great moral evil that it was, had become stale.

'It's meant to be a powerful parable, I know,' he said. 'Powerful against organised prejudice in the world.'

True. It was. In a world where very few things gather any sort of consensus around them as either right or wrong, the Holocaust is wrong, yes. School kids across the land are even now writing angry essays about how unfair it was.

'But it has become wallpaper, frankly,' he continued. 'It doesn't transform anyone. Remembering it doesn't prevent xenophobia; hearing about it doesn't promote religious tolerance; teaching it doesn't reduce social injustice. It is a symbol with its bollocks quietly airbrushed out, basically. Children denounce it at ten o'clock in the classroom, and shout "Black bastard" in the playground at eleven. I know. I lived in the playground. Monuments are only built by the powerful, anyway.'

'Sorry?'

'Erecting monuments to the victims of past atrocities. They always come too late. Once a social group are able to demand and have built a monument, they're powerful. Once a social group are a party piece of moral concern, feted by celebrities who need to feel better about the large sums of money in their account – then they probably don't need a monument any more. Their battle for recognition is already won. They're mainstream, assimilated, fashionable. When they needed a monument, it wasn't there. Now they don't, it is. That's how

it is for the dispossessed. When they most need a saviour, a saviour isn't there. When they need a celebrity,
they're just not around. When they need a press campaign, the journalists are all still working on the story
before. When they need a witness, there's no one. So
they die alone. They die unrecognised. They die
unheard. And the meaninglessness of it all is completely underwhelming. Nice show though, Jenny.'

Nice show. It was just as well he'd enjoyed it. For he
was the catalyst ensuring there wouldn't be many more.
The bottom began to fall out of everything. If this
ground wasn't solid, what was? Suddenly my morality
was looking tired, a little paint-by-numbers. It was a
piece of fruit from which all the juice had been
squeezed. Here comes the millennium and I didn't have
anything to say. A joke for every occasion but a message for none. I was the stand-up who'd had to sit
down. I was the stand-up who'd had to reinvent herself
and become quirky for telly instead. And right now I
was the stand-up on her knees, crawling towards the
prosecution. Towards Little. Towards the child. The
children. The Lost Children. Who before they died,
and if it was all right everybody else, just wanted to
know what the hell was going on.

I couldn't turn round in the tunnel. That was the
worst thing. Or one of the worst things. It was pretty

full of worst things in fact. There was a bit of queue of
them all jostling for place. But not being able to turn
round was *one* of the worst things. I was committed to
going forward. Initially the slope was slightly down-
wards. My shoulders brushed against the side walls.
Had Little really come this way? What would make
someone come this way out of choice? You'd have to be
very desperate. Then my hands and knees were in some
water which freaked me. Was the tunnel filling up? Was
the tide coming in? The first incoming tide in the history of the Sahara. Call me a trifle unlucky. I stopped
and listened. I could hear the occasional drip. But no
torrent. Not even a trickle. And alone in the deepest
dark of the earth's core, I felt my hearing was good.
Sharp. Maybe I wasn't drowning. Maybe if I just kept
calm, just breathed steadily, just held on – it would be
all right. I edged forward. If the water got deeper then
I was in trouble. It was half way up my arms. Would I
be prepared to swim forward? Launch myself into
unknown water? Cold unknown water. It was cold.
Cavern cold. And for a moment I desired it. I'll swim to
the centre of the earth, to the core of the madness, and
then dip my head under and never return. But at least I
would have got to the heart of the matter. Then I'd
know. Then I'd be certain. What was what. Who was
what. Why was what …

But the slope seemed to be upwards and I felt I was leaving the water behind. Hard to tell, because I was wet and chilled, despite my sweat and my knees were sore. I paused to listen. Nothing. And nothing to see either. Up ahead, there was nothing to see but darkness. How far would I travel before giving up? How much do you have to care before you say 'No more?' Would I go ten more yards and then inch myself backwards towards the porch? Would I go twenty yards? A hundred yards? How would I know? Who would tell me? Who would say, 'Enough's enough'? No one. It was down to me. It was about what I wanted. And how much I wanted it. That was the worst thing.

This was some womb. And in the unknowing and relentless black, I sensed Sian. Began to speak with her. This was her territory after all. She knew about this. She knew about a darkness with no exit, no light at the end of the tunnel. You know *all* about this, don't you, my little angel? And now I'm here. They've allowed me to visit. I've come to see you. It's been a while, I know. But I'm here for you now, my little darling. You never got beyond this. I haven't forgotten. Well, I had forgotten. I never really knew. Never really thought. I'm sorry. Sorry that I never wanted to hold you. I stood in the light you never reached, but I couldn't hold you. Sorry that I let them take over, and take you away.

Because I wanted you above all things. Can you hear me? Just say if you can. Just speak. Speak to mummy. She's come to find you. I understand the darkness now. I understand it. I feel it. And if this is the end, then at least – at least we've been together in a way. Do you feel that? Not what it might have been. We might have played in the sand. Actually, I hate sand. But the pier maybe. Yes. We could have shared an ice cream on the pier at Southend. Gazed into the rock pools. Argued about the homework, argued about the parties, fallen out over pocket money and getting your nose pierced. But on Saturday mornings you might sometimes have sat on my bed, before growing up and growing away. You would have grown away, of course. But then grown back? Maybe. But I always would have been there and you would have been there, your picture on the side, several of them, growing up, that's my daughter, I would have said, and we could have met for lunch on a spare Monday and gone to the National, and Trafalgar Square before we said goodbye at Leicester Square tube. But we said goodbye long before we got there. Or rather, we didn't.

The silence. The sigh and silence of the alone. The silence of the sad, of the longing. Just the darkness. Light. Almost blinding. Flickering light. Candle light. Ahead. I saw it. Through the tears, salty light. Blurred light. I'd reached the Tomb. Had I? Was this the Tomb? Was this the end? I scrambled the last two metres. Loving the light. And then the small flickering face. Little.

'What is it that you want?' she asked.

*

If only he'd been sitting the other side of the doctor. If only the underwear hadn't caught Abbot Peter's eye. But he wasn't and it had, and it was orange, and the whole therapeutic process was in jeopardy.

Abbot Peter was doing his best. He was sitting with Dr James and trying not to look at the doctor's jacket pocket. For just peaking over the lip of the pocket were the pants. The underpants previously worn on the head. They were bright orange. The bright orange pants previously worn over the head of the man who was now seeing him in a professional capacity. His healer, in fact. His healer sometimes wore his pants on his head, although at this particular time, they were in his jacket pocket, stuffed there no doubt amidst the reverie of last night. And the Abbot was in a dilemma. He was remembering what Musselly said about how important it was that there would be no recriminations in the morning; that these high-powered people should be able to come and enjoy themselves without the sense that anyone was looking on. So obviously he wasn't going to mention the pants. Don't mention the pants. That much was clear. Pants? What pants? But it was also clear to Peter that they weren't helping the therapeutic process. He *should* have been getting in touch with his feelings for that strange nanny his family had once hired when he was five. Instead, however, caught in the thrall of the underwear before his eyes, he was in touch only with 'The good ship, *Venus*'. Verse five mainly.

And there was another problem. One of concern. From the way the good doctor moved in his slightly course cloth trousers on his prickly wicker chair, it was apparent that he wasn't wearing any underpants. And that he was suffering. The pants in his pocket were clearly the only pair he'd travelled with. The clarity of Peter's thought was frightening. And until the good doctor found his pants, there was some tickly-prickly discomfort to be had. A word from Peter and the suffering could be lessened. 'Excuse me, but your pants are in your pocket.' But would that be a word too far? Would the whole dynamic of the therapeutic process be overthrown? For what would happen then? If the doctor left the room to put them on, how could he return with dignity? If he didn't leave, but dropped his trousers then and there, hobbled about on one leg briefly as he got his other leg in, how could he continue with dignity? What would he say to restore things?

No, on this particular morning, the therapeutic process was stuttering a little. But Abbot Peter knew one thing. He knew that he mustn't mention the pants. Whatever else he knew, he knew that. Mustn't even allude to them. Talk about anything, but not that. The doctor's private life was his affair. Last night was his affair. He'd enjoyed himself. He'd relaxed. Lovely, super, wonderful, brilliant, marvellous. No mention of anything the morning after.

'You seem to find it hard to look me in the eye,' said the doctor. 'Is it misplaced guilt?'

'No. It's your pants,' said Peter.

★

Meanwhile, Rowena had been counting and so far it was 478, which is a lot of skulls. A lot of skulls to dust down and move to the other side of the corridor. Archbishop Musselly had particularly asked her to do this, though. It was, apparently, done every fifty years as regular as clockwork. And she wasn't really in a position to argue, since she wasn't really a nun and she didn't really exist. Her room was free because no one else wanted it, basically. And no one else wanted it because they didn't want to walk past hundreds of skulls ten times a day, and dispute space with the original desert rats.

So the Archbishop had said she could come and stay

a while. That was six years ago now. Everyone assumed she was a member of some particularly holy order of St So-and-so. But she wasn't. She was instead, a member of the holy order of normal people who have to eke out an existence in the normal world, the secular world, without hundreds of services every day to support them. Her most recent job had been in Administration and Personnel for a large joiners. She'd run the place. She'd enjoyed her £27,000 p.a. and enjoyed her flat in St Albans. Here, however, she was a free-loader, really. Not officially a man. Not officially on the books. And not officially in a position to argue when asked to move the skulls.

A candle burnt next to her, for today was the fourth anniversary of the death of Tom. She talked as she worked. Talked with Tom. The skulls were those of the monks who had lived and served in this place down the centuries. So a strong sense of communion with the past wasn't hard to create. They had stood where she stood now. They had moved the skulls as she moved them now. And then, when the shades had lengthened for them; when the changes and chances of this fleeting world had left them spent and exhausted; when their little day was over and their small work done, they'd joined the pile, as maybe one day she would. Unofficially, of course.

From Exploitation to Contemplation. The Fourth Mystical Path. The move from seeing everything and everyone as there to be used; to seeing everything and everyone as there to be wondered at; held, not in captivity or contempt, but in awe. Even the rats. Even the rats, who, despite constant reassurances and ultimatums had never quite got around to moving out. Extraordinary animals, rats. There was much to be in awe of, frankly. On arriving in England in the eighteenth century, the brown rat had been the ultimate ethnic minority. No room at the inn, so they were taken round the back and given the sewers to live in. Instead of grumbling, they said, fine and by the nineteenth century had made a huge success out of sewer life. They could run a hundred metres in less than ten seconds and could stay afloat in water for seventy-two hours. Admittedly, they carried disease but were less life-threatening in this department than town pigeons. Not generally much bigger than hamsters, the largest being the length of a man's forearm from head to tail, they just *seemed* bigger. They were the only small furry animal people loved to hate. No horror film was complete without them. But neither was any laboratory. The revenge of the human, when in the end, like everybody else, all the rat wanted was food and a home. Like Rowena. And St Raphael's for her was a sort of homecoming.

From Exploitation to Contemplation. The Mystic Paths were reassuringly practical, basic and every day. You could have your favourites, of course. But all were important. You couldn't pick and choose, for each cured in a different way. Today, however, she wouldn't exploit. Today, she would attempt simple awe. She would contemplate the skulls. She would even contemplate the rats. She could manage that. Contemplating living human beings was obviously the ultimate challenge.

*

The following morning, Abbot Peter said goodbye to St Raphael's. He was returning to St James the Less, to resume his abbot duties. Before he went, a little bit of physical exertion to be undertaken, but that wouldn't take long. Meanwhile, Fr Lopez got up from his desk in the library, put away his glasses, stretched, got cramp in his right leg, and decided to go for a walk. Whilst not seventy metres away, Ted Delbaba's feet would shortly leave the ground. No helicopter involved. Just Archbishop Mussely. Up, up and away but Ted wouldn't be singing. Ted would be screaming. Screaming for dear life. No one knew it, but there was a finale in the dry desert air ...

CHAPTER NINE

Happy?

'Do you think I will always be unhappy?' asked Little. 'No reason why you should be, no. It's very hard growing up.'

'Van Gogh was always unhappy.'

What could I say? Little was right. He was always unhappy really. Even when he was happy, he was unhappy. The straggly plant had never recovered. Never recovered from the stunting, deforming early frost. Born the son of Theodorus, the 'handsome parson' who couldn't preach, and Anna, the kind and respected bookseller's daughter, he never quite made it to happiness. His unrequited love in Brixton for Eugenie, his landlady's daughter, was a dry run for a series of disastrous and painful relationships with women. He either sought to be mothered or play the mother. Neither worked.

He always managed to choose the uninterested or the unreachable or the impossible.

It was in Arles that he painted 'The cafe terrace at night'. He was very pleased with it, for it was a night picture in which there was no black: 'nothing but beautiful blue and violet and green and in those surroundings the lighted square is coloured limey yellow and sulphur green.' A night picture with no black. The black he saved for within. He would save the world with pictures of hope, yellow hope, sunflower hope. But he couldn't save himself. He would paint light like no other; light which stunned his eyes and warmed his back, but never quite reached his soul. His would always be an unquiet soul. There'd be no rest this side of the grave. Hence that question. The question knocking on the door of heaven and waiting for an answer. The question posed by Monet and echoed by Little: How could a man who so loved flowers and light, and rendered them so well, have managed to be so unhappy?

'Good artist though!'

'But a sad one. And I'm just wondering if I'll be like that. Always sad. I don't want always to be sad.'

'But you must enjoy some things.'

'Sometimes I think I do, but then I look back on them, and wonder if I did. Sometimes I smile when I'm not happy. I do that quite a lot.'

What to say? I was no child psychologist. Didn't really know any children well.

'What do you like doing?' I asked.

'I like dressing up,' she said.

'Do you?'

'Sometimes. Not always.'

'But sometimes. For parties, special occasions?'

'Yes,' she said with a glimmer of a smile, and a flicker of a hope, and the furtive look of a secret shared. Someone else knew now. She liked dressing up.

'I like dressing up and looking in the mirror.'

'We'll have to arrange something. Something for you to dress up for. With a mirror, of course.'

'There is nothing. There's nothing to dress up for.'

The glimmer and the flicker were gone.

'We could have a party. When's your birthday?'

'Not for ages.'

That figured. When you're sitting at the core of the earth in a cave called the Tomb, you must expect the problems to be pretty intractable. Problems which weren't intractable wouldn't have got this far. They would have been knocked out in the qualifying stages. This was Wembley. This was the Centre Court at Wimbledon. This was the Crucible in Sheffield. This was Crufts. And this was the Final. This was not territory where a couple of aspirins or a good idea were going to be very healing.

'Right. So it's a special This-is-*not*-my-birthday party! What's your favourite food?'

Little smiled. But it wasn't a smile from laughter within. It was a smile out of pity for my lack of understanding; out of kindness that I was at least trying; but out of a deep knowing that I was scraping around as deep as I could go and only managing to reach the surface.

'The important thing is not to worry. Whatever you find inside you, don't worry. It can't hurt you. You're safe.'

I was stealing Abbot Peter's lines unashamedly but I couldn't think of anything else to say.

'What do you mean?'

Good question. What did I mean? More importantly, what did Abbot Peter mean? They were his words. He was the one who believed them. I was just passing them on. The messenger. You don't ask the poor messenger what the message means. It's meant to be obvious. Otherwise, what's the point of the message?

'I mean that you're safe. You needn't worry about what you find, because you're safe. You're loved.'

'I don't know if I am. I don't think he does.'

'Who?'

'Maybe in his own way. But he doesn't show it.'

'God?'

'My dad.'

124

'Oh. Who is your dad?'

'He works here.'

'I see.'

Well, this certainly put the cat among the pigeons, and no mistake. Her dad worked here? In the monastery? So one of the permanent staff had a secret. I could see Poirot even now, standing arm on lectern in the chapel, declaring that the father of this child was in this very room, whilst the camera worked numerous close-ups on faces of distraught and aghast monks. 'Oh yes, I think so,' Poirot would say, giving his moustache and outrageous accent a little tweak. 'I must admit, for a long time I was blind – blinded by the sand being thrown in my eyes. Hercule Poirot suffers the desert blindness. Things were not clear. There was grit in the grey cells. No one was quite what they seemed. I experienced the, how you say, mirage, yes? Take Archbishop Musselly, for instance.'

'Me, Poirot? But that's ridiculous!'

'Is it? I wonder, Archbishop. That title – so impressive. But titles – they can cover a multitude of sins, I think.'

And Poirot would be away, working his way around the group until the final revelation …

'Hang on a sec,' I said to Little. 'I've got something in my pocket. A piece of paper. Do you know what a mystic is?'

'Someone who's a bit religious and a bit nutty? Talks to plants.'

'That's right. Well, before I left to come and find you, this woman gave me a special message. Shall we see if we can make some sense of it? Might be in code.'

'All right.'

Little didn't seem very convinced but it was something to do, which was the only reason why I suggested it. Might give me time to work out what to do next. Like how to get her out of here. How to get her to leave. I was working hard in my mind on that one.

'I'm not leaving here, you know,' she said.

'Who's asking you to leave?' I said.

'You will soon.'

Question: what's the point of me having secret thoughts if everyone in this place seems to know what I'm thinking already?

'Well, you and I – we'll obviously have to leave eventually, yes. I mean, with no food or water, we'll die here.'

'I think so, yes.'

'What d'you mean, you think so?'

'I think I want to die here.'

What?!

'Let's look in my pocket,' I said.

The water had been deeper than I thought. The paper was sodden. The writing unreadable. The Fourth

Mystical Path was a complete wash-out. It was water-logged. Impassable. Which meant that my delaying tactics had failed and I might just have to face the truth, which I, like the rest of humanity, found very difficult.

'Just supposing you were unhappy for the rest of your life. Is that a reason to throw it away?'

'Could be. I don't want to be unhappy any more.'

'No.'

Nor did I. Nor does anyone. We needed something fresh here.

'Shouldn't think Van Gogh did either,' I added. 'Shouldn't think he enjoyed being unhappy. But he did paint some pretty brilliant paintings along the way. Perhaps he wasn't as unhappy as some people have made out.'

'No, he was. He painted things he couldn't feel himself, you see. It was like he was painting from somewhere else. Somewhere which wasn't inside him. From a dream, from a longing, from a rainbow. But he never felt it himself. He was always unhappy.'

'What's your dream, Little?'

'I'd like to live by myself, have a big sofa, and run a hairdresser's.'

Talking of hairdressers, I was very conscious that my roots were beginning to show, but there wasn't a lot I could do about that now.

'And could unhappy people come there?'

'Oh, yes. I'd understand, you see.'

'That's one of the good things about sadness, I suppose. It can be turned into different things. It can be turned into paintings which move people; or hairdressers who can help people.'

'Are you sad sometimes?'

'I'm one of those people who prefer not to think about it too much.'

'Why not?'

'I just don't. I prefer to get on with things. Forget.'

'But how can you forget you're sad?'

'By keeping busy. Working hard. Doing things.'

'What do you do?'

'I tell jokes.'

'But what do you do for a job?'

'I tell jokes. That is my job.'

'Funny job for a sad person.'

'Not really.'

'But how can you tell jokes if you're sad?'

'Because a lot of jokes are quite sad, too.'

'Tell me a sad joke.'

Oh, dear. Rule number one. Never analyse comedy. But I wasn't going to get out of this.

'What do you call a fly with no wings?'

'I don't know.'

'A walk.'

'I don't understand.'

'No. Well, you're not the first.'

'Explain it.'

'I won't explain it, no. Sorry. But it's a rule I have. Never explain jokes. Because no one ever laughed at an explanation.'

'Oh, go on.'

'No. But one day you'll get it. One day, you'll be opening up at your hair salon and it will suddenly happen for you and you'll be chuckling for the rest of the day.'

'I doubt it.'

'Encouraging, aren't you?'

'Anyway, if it's as sad as you say, why laugh? What's funny about sadness?'

'You're a real professor of impossibly hard questions this morning.'

'Well, you said there was nothing to worry about. Whatever I found inside wasn't anything to worry about. That I was safe. You said that.'

Bugger. Why wasn't she talking to Fr Kolbe, instead of five generations of atheism? Someone to talk of the journey into love and darkness. Someone to say that we can laugh at sad jokes because they're not the end of the story. That our dreams and longings are true. Somewhere, they're true. That perhaps the big starry nights on Vincent's canvas really did lead somewhere. That there was a beyond. And that even if the fly was reduced to a walk these days, it didn't mean he always would be. One day, in some glorious paradise, he would fly again.

Instead, she was talking to me. Daddy's girl. And every hopeful word I uttered seemed to hurt him. It was for the kid, I reassured myself. You say anything to the figure on the ledge, eleven storeys above the shopping mall below. You say anything and everything. Don't jump. Stay exactly where you are. It's OK. It's all right. It can be sorted. It's not as bad as you think. Of course you do. Then you get them down and obviously it isn't OK and it isn't all right, and it probably is as bad as they think, if not worse, but at least they haven't splattered themselves everywhere. It's all right, dad. I'll stay faithful. I will. I won't let you down. You know that I always said I'd never let you down, and I never will. That's what I'd said, when I threw the rose on the coffin. And rose promises you keep. But sometimes it's hard having no hope.

'You're coming with me, and we're going in search of the big sofa. And when we've found that, we'll have to start thinking about the hairdressing. Yes?'

We were both very cold. And I dreaded the idea of returning through the tunnel. But not in the same way as I had before. At least this time I knew where I was heading.

'Yes?'

'Yes what?'

'Coming?'

'You don't understand, do you?' said Little.

No, I didn't really. We sat for a while in the semi-gloom. Chill.

'And do you have a name yet?' I asked after a few empty minutes.

'Why?'

'Well, because names matter. It's important that some-one knows your name.'

'I've told God.'

'OK.'

'Just now. I told God my name. I want to see if it makes a difference.'

'Fine.'

'So what do you think about that?'

'I think it's a very good idea.'

'Do you?'

'Oh, yes. Very good idea.'

'So have you done it?'

'Done what?'

'Told God your name.'

Questions. So many questions. Avoid.

'I was rather hoping God knew my name already,' I said.

'Wasn't what I asked.'

'No. But it's what I answered.'

Pause. Sometimes we said the Lord's Prayer when I was at primary school. It was my first, last and only religious instruction. In the early days I found it completely incomprehensible. We used to make up different versions. Sarah's amendments to the opening lines I always found strangely compelling: 'Our Father, who shouts in heaven, "Hullo! What's your name?"' I'd never told him, though. It would have been a major betrayal of my family and, anyway, God had bigger fish to fry. Like the small question of his non-existence. Brisk change of subject necessary here.

'Now – how do you feel about a return journey through the tunnel?'

'No chance.'

'We'll have to. I don't like it any more than you, but at least we know it's leading us to safety.'

'You can't get back through the tunnel. It's one-way. The way the rock is formed. You'd be cut to shreds. That's why it's called the Tomb.'

'Don't be ridiculous. Of course we can get back.'

I got up, taking the candle with me. Little didn't move. I peered into the darkness, into the tunnel, into the pathway home. And felt fairly ill. Nauseous. Little was right. The way the stones were laid at an angle. I hadn't noticed. Looking at it from here though, every stone was a knife aimed at the knees and hands of anyone foolish enough to attempt a crawl. They let you in. But they didn't let you out. So why hadn't Abbot Peter stopped me? Would have been a sight more valuable than telling me not to worry, that I was safe. But then, of course, he was a visitor here, too. He probably didn't know. He probably thought the Tomb was a quaint little tourist stunt just like I did. How was he to know that once inside, that was that?

The Tomb. I was in my tomb. Inevitable, I suppose, but I had rather been hoping that on reaching my tomb, I might be dead on arrival. It was traditional. And in the meantime, it might have been kind, thoughtful and indeed life-saving if someone had put a warning at the head of the tunnel: 'This is Not A Game. This is One-Way.' But then if it was called the Tomb, perhaps that was rather taken for granted. Onewayness was a feature of most tombs. An unspoken assumption. They lowered you in and that was that. They didn't expect to see you back three days later with interesting stories of your time there and photos to match. It wasn't like a long weekend in Paris. It was final. It was One-Way. Tombs were tombs. It was just that – well, I didn't want to die.

'Told you,' said Little.

'Not exactly Madcap Marjorie of the Upper Fifth, are you?'

'What do you mean?'

'Madcap Marjorie, fearless and frantic, who's always up for another rippingly exciting adventure. You're hardly that, are you? You've given up.'

I was seething. I was terrified.

'I gave up a long time ago,' said Little in a voice that really irritated me.

'There has to be another way,' I said.

'I haven't found it.'

'Have you looked?'

'Not really. There used to be an exit behind us, I think, but it's filled by stone now.'

I was running through the options in my mind. It didn't take long. There weren't any. As I understood it, *we* couldn't get out, and no adult of any size could get *in*. And if anyone *did* get in, whatever size, *they* couldn't get out, unless accompanied by a large slab of Semtex which would do a lot more damage to us than it would to the rock. Welcome to the Tomb.

I could feel the crack Little was talking about. At least I thought I could. But there was no sense of exit there. No give. No feeling that if I just pushed a little harder the earth would begin to move. Solid rock. I banged at it with a stone. Banged hard again and again and again. Pointless. I shouted. Quietly at first, quiet shouting, because I couldn't get away from the idea that I was standing in a church and that in a moment, the verger would be up alongside me, asking me to keep my voice down. But in the apparent absence of the verger, I began to get more confident. Noisy shouting. I quite enjoyed it. It seemed to get something out of my system. But again, of course, it was pointless.

Meanwhile, the prosecution sat motionless on the ground, making me feel foolish. Just another washed up and useless adult. I held the candle slightly higher. There was a small hole in the roof of the cave. But no light came through it. And no one other than one of the smaller members of the Dwarf Sparrow family could possibly squeeze through. Fr Kolbe never got out. They let him in. But they carried him out.

'I'm cold,' said Little.

'When did you last sleep?'

'I don't know.'

'We'll huddle together and sleep and when we wake up –'

'We won't wake up.'

'Of course we will.'

'It's too cold. I can't feel below my knees. And anyway – there's nothing to wake for and nowhere to go to. The crows are gathering.'

Maybe she was right. I hadn't realised how cold I was until she mentioned it. And at least I'd found her. She wouldn't die alone now. Not like Sian. She'd die with me. We'd die together. I'd done what I set out to do. I couldn't do more than that. What did I expect, a medal or something? A shiny public service gong and a generous pension? After all, I wasn't a civil servant.

'Let's sit over here. We can huddle together.'

And so we did. We found a natural corner where we could wedge ourselves in. Our cold bodies came together and made for a little warmth. I remember her breathing deepening. She was exhausted. We'd be found together in a hundred years, our skeletons entwined. And they'd say, at least they died together. Mother and daughter. Quite sweet in its way. And then the candle went out. I don't know for how long it had burned, but it flickered and was gone. And I watched the darkness where it had been. The darkness hadn't put it out. But it quickly moved in where the light had been. I felt the oblivion. I felt the wall. It was full of dirty cracks. Wouldn't mind, but I'd heard them all before. Boom, boom. Old habits die hard. The jokes kept coming. And I thought of Abbot Peter and his sausage, and wondered if sausages were still funny in a tomb. Less so, I felt. Once the candle's gone out, jokes suddenly become very lonely and rather insecure. They were really only meant for the candle light, because they can only travel whilst accompanied by hope. They can't walk very far alone. So no more jokes now, Jenny, because the light was gone. Just put them down. They're over. We won't gather lilacs in the spring again. And we won't walk together down an English lane. That's it. Jokes aren't us any more. Might have been nice, though, to bow out on one with a slightly shorter and more glorious history ...

But the trouble was that apart from jokes, I didn't have a lot else. I didn't have the Mass, for instance, nor hundreds of psalms. I just had the darkness, and the stillness and the silence. I had Little, of course. And I had the warmth which she gave me. I was tired. I tapped the wall behind three times. It must be about time for the genie to make an appearance. Tap, tap, tap. And Hey Presto! Nothing. Not a sausage. Ah! The sausage again. It obviously doesn't know that comedy died two minutes ago. Could someone tell the sausage, please. I haven't the heart. There's nothing like being in control, and this was nothing like being in control ... was that a gag? ... No, I think that was serious. So hard to tell sometimes ... strangely peaceful though ... maybe there was nothing to worry about. Maybe I was safe. Or maybe I was delirious, because I could face anything and everything except the fact that everything I'd ever done and hoped for was finally adding up to this.

I lay there for hours. Minutes even. Could someone explain how time works? I was cold ...

CHAPTER TEN

Losing Control

'**H**AVE you gone completely mad?' screamed Ted.

'No,' said Musselly, looking down into the desperate eyes of the man he was holding over the balcony of the basilica. Beneath them, a seventy-foot drop, and a group of increasingly interested sightseers busily flicking through their guide books to see which particular tradition at St Raphael's they were now watching. 'No, I've gone completely sane. That's why I find you so offensive.'

'You do know that the millennium deal is off. It's off, mate. I'm pulling out. We've got a site on Chatham Islands anyway. Did I forget to mention that? Careless of me. So you can whistle for your money now, bristlehead. But it'll need to be a bloody good tune to raise what you need. You've missed the boat badly.'

'And you've missed the point, Ted. Because you'll be dead by the millennium. Indeed, you'll be dead by evening prayer. So come the glorious millennial dawn, you'll have been six foot under for some time, and looking a lot less than your best. Three sunrises? You won't even see tomorrow's.'

Musselly's strong hands each held a wrist of Ted, whilst Ted's hands sought out all the support they could find round Musselly's wrists. But amidst the strength and the grip, sweat was beginning to trickle and loosen.

'Mind you, nor will I,' continued Musselly. 'More's the shame, because I love a good dawn but no, my sunrises will probably be limited, too. I'll probably be in prison for your murder. But that's all right. I'm used to institutional life. And who knows, it might be a room with a view.'

'Jesus Christ!'

'Jesus Christ? Now there's a name from the past. Or is it the future? Or is it both? So confusing. Still, I'm sure you'll meet him one way or another. Quite soon, in fact. Though obviously traditional notions of time rather break down after physical death, so when I say "soon" it might be in a thousand million years, but *seem* soon, if you see what I mean. Anyway, it might be worth you thinking about your opening lines even now.

First impressions are *so* important, don't you think? And we wouldn't want him to get the *wrong* one. He's very understanding, of course. Meek and mild and all that. Like me, really. But if you think the shadow of Mount Sinai is frightening, you should see Jesus when confronted by someone who pisses on others. And who doesn't stop when challenged about it.'

'Get real, you sad man. You're not going to let me go. And I'm not going to let you go. We'll be back inside in a couple of minutes and you'll be taken away in a strait jacket to a safe place.'

'I'd prefer my strait jacket to the body bag you'll be in.'

'Is this the only way you can get attention these days?'

'So before I do let go of you, and watch you tumble, I was just wondering if there was anything you wanted to say. Last words and all that. Final messages to the planet you've so abused?'

'I can't believe this.'

'I was just wondering if you wanted to apologise, for instance?'

'Apologise?'

'Yes. It means saying sorry. Unfamiliar territory for you, but not unknown in these parts.'

'Apologise for what?'

'Screwing people? You could start with that. Why

not? You could start with that, and then move on to other areas. Often it's the starting which is the hard bit. The first sorry. But then it does get easier. You sort of get into the rhythm. Don't you find that? I do, Ted.'

'I've nothing to apologise for.'

'Oh, dear. Dear, oh, dear. Deary, deary me. I hate it when people say that. "I've got nothing to apologise for." The unexamined life. Nightmare. Because not even God can make anything of that.'

'We're all out there making a living.'

'Certainly.'

'Rats in a bag.'

'Ah, no. That's where we part. We're not rats in a bag, Ted. Not rats in a bag, but people sharing a table. We're people sharing a table and trying to make sure that everyone has enough to eat. It's a meal, Ted. And your table manners are a nightmare.'

'You're a relic, aren't you?'

'I like to think so, yes. Relics are important. Lose touch with the past, and you really are up shit creek.'

'I hope they put you away for ever.'

There was a pause. Each man's hand continued to grip around the wrists of the other. But strength ebbed, sweat flowed and chests heaved in the dry desert air. Gently, the first sign of fear appeared in Ted's eyes.

'Pull me up, you bastard.'

'Why?'

'Because this is going to change nothing.'

'It's altering your day a little.'

'You're sick.'

'I don't know if you've had a good day so far or not, Ted. How's it been? A bit of this and a bit of that? I expect so. Trouble is, however it's been, it's downhill from here as far as you're concerned. I mean, even if it's been a bad day, it's downhill from here. Literally. You've had the best of it. Maybe you didn't realise that at the time, but you have. You were so busy cutting your deals that you were completely blind to the moment. And then, suddenly, here we are, and it's slowly beginning to dawn on you that those moments were it. Those moments were all you had. Don't look down by the way. It won't reassure you. There's a lot of space between you and the ground.'

'Typical of the Church. When all else fails, use terror. You get out the fires of hell and try to frighten.'

'Who mentioned hell? As far as I remember, the only person I mentioned was Jesus.'

'Look, understand this. We're not frightened anymore. None of us. No one believes you, you see.'

'Of course not. But just tell me one thing before we part. What guided you, Ted? The camel is guided by a thin wooden stick, that we both know. But what guided you? What guided you to this point?'

'Pull me up, Musselly. I can't hold on for much longer. You've done what you wanted. You've given me a fright.'

'And you've given me nothing.'

'No one gave me anything.'

'Sorry?'

'No one gave me anything. If I have anything now it's because I went out and got it. No one gave me *nothing*. D'you understand?'

'Ah. The nerve of this discomfiture. Is that what you feel?'

Each held the gaze of the other …

*

Sunlight in the desert isn't a surprising thing, but it is when you're dead. Or presumed dead. And that's what I presumed myself to be. But I was lying on rock, and there was some scuffling around me, and there was some sunlight in my eyes if I cared to open them, which I did, to find Merrybum leaning over me, listening for life. I took hold of his ear.

'What are you doing?'

'I'm feeling a bit of a novice.'

Comedy was back. Not great comedy, but please – I'd been dead for God knows how long.

'This is no time for jokes. We thought you were dead.'

'No time for jokes? This is exactly the time for jokes. I can explain.'

'Later. We're a bit worried about Little.'

'Is she all right?'

'She was very cold.'

'Was?'

'Yes. But we think she's all right.'

'Only think.'

'We're not doctors. I was an accountant –'

'You mentioned.'

'But she's breathing. And it's steady breathing.'

Relief. Huge relief. More relief at her being alive than myself, which was completely unbelievable but true. I'd made it. I'd got there. I'd shared it. I'd done something. I raised myself up on my elbow, and there she was, lying a few feet from me. Fr Lopez was at her side.

'Little?' I said.

She lay quiet. She was nearer to the Tomb than me. I could see behind her the forced, rock-smashed hole which must have been our exit. Stony rubble. Dark inside. But fresh desert air outside, and light. Such light.

'My name's Hatchesput,' she said.

'Hatchesput?'

'Hatchesput. Most people call me Hatch.'

Then I'll call you Hatch. There's nothing to worry about. We're safe.'

'Fascinating,' said Fr Lopez, his eyes dancing something between the quick-step and the fox-trot.

'Really?'

'She ruled for twenty years or so towards the end of the fourteenth century BC,' he added.

'Who did?'

'The original Hatchesput. One of the very few female Egyptian pharaohs. Called the "bearded lady" because she was regularly portrayed dressed as a king, with pleated kilt, bare chest and false beard. Yes, sad story, really. She was no saint, of course. She had a habit of borrowing military victories from her predecessor. Falsifying public records. His victories became hers. But that was nothing to what was perpetrated on her death, when someone – probably her stepson Tuthmosis the Third – did everything possible to erase her memory. Very vindictive. Not nice at the best of times but particularly spiteful in Egypt, of course, because the preservation of the ancient Egyptian's name in this world was the very key to their survival in the next. But there we are. It was done. People can be ever so cruel. Paintings of her were defaced, reliefs of her as king were attacked with chisels, and hundreds of statues of her were smashed to pieces and buried. Wretched business. Quite wretched.'

I'd heard of women borrowing party dresses. But not military victories. I could see her now ferreting around in the drawers of history, and suddenly there it was. A military victory to die for. She would whip it out, and standing in front of the mirror with it, she would shout to Osipsus, 'Come and have a look at this one! It's gorgeous!' And Osipsus would come running and say how much it suited Madam, and Hatchesput would say, yes she thought so too, especially as apparently there were 60,000 dead by the end of the fight, and Osipsus would add that there *were* those who put the figure at *100,000* dead, at which Hatchesput would squeal with delight, tell Osipsus that he said the kindest things, and run off to let her maid know of her discovery ...

'So how come we're alive?' I asked.

'Through extraordinary luck,' said Fr Lopez, 'and Novice Merrybum's strong arms.'

'He's the hero,' said Merrybum. 'He heard you shouting. Made a fair old din. Enough to wake the Sphinx. There's clearly built in amplification in the rock.'

I thought of the Dwarf Sparrow hole. With feeling. Small is beautiful. Small is big.

'I never usually come this way on my walk. But today I did. I'd got cramp in the library. Needed a stretch. There was a lot of rock to be moved, of course. But Merry stuck at it, hammered, cracked and heaved away. Even carried a little rubble myself, which for an eminent historian ...'

'Clearly there had been an entrance there once,' continued Merrybum, picking up the story from his Eminence. 'but it was filled by one particularly large stone. Who knows how long you might have been in there ...'

'Abbot Peter knew where I was.'

'Abbot Peter left yesterday. Yesterday morning. Long before we knew you were missing. You must remember, it has been a busy time for us here.'

'Too busy to care for a guest? Too busy to have your eyes open for a child?'

'We do our best.'

'Not from where I'm lying. How long were we in there?'

'Forty-eight hours?'

'Forty-eight hours? Thanks for nothing. We could have died in there. I can't believe it.'

I hated myself for getting caught up in this ritual. I looked across at the empty Tomb and wondered what I'd learned. I'd learned that I didn't want to die again for a while, if that was all right with everyone else. And I'd learned that I hated losing control. But I'd also learned something else. I'd learned that I was a good person. I'd never realised that before. But I was. I was a good person, a brave person because I'd gone in after Little, even though I was terrified. That took courage and it took goodness. So why was I behaving like a shit?

'I'm sorry,' I said.

'It's all right,' said Lopez. 'None of us is proud about what happened.'

That just made me feel worse and the whole wretchedness of everything welled up inside me.

'It's me. I come from a culture, you see, where we have to blame someone; it helps us to believe we're in control. Funny, but true. The insecure need to pretend control. Means that when things go wrong, the ritual of blame is important. Very important. Crucial. If we can identify a culprit, and lay the blame fairly and squarely at their door, and make them feel really bad, we not only make ourselves feel self-righteously good – we can also almost convince ourselves that this breakdown of order won't happen again; that it was a blip and not the norm; that we really are in control. It was *their* fault but now it's sorted. Yes. They're guilty. They're punished. And we're back in control. Things should be OK from here on. But we're not. And they aren't. They're never OK from here on. This is white-water rafting with no rudder and a mere stick for a paddle.'

I paused and looked into the sky. No crows over the wheatfield at the moment. Not for me anyway. They were out there for someone on this planet right now, but not as yet for me. Yet I longed for a definite voice. I longed for a confident truth.

'Tell me I'm wrong,' I said. 'Tell me we are.'

'Tell you we are what?'

'In control.'

'In control?'

'Yes.'

'No. I can't. Or rather, only of certain things. As you said, even amidst the white water, we do have a thin stick.'

'I suppose you're going to say that everyone can at least seek God.'

'No. To be honest I was going to ignore your ramblings, and suggest you drank something. You're probably quite dehydrated still.'

'Don't worry. I don't mind you mentioning God. I mean, you are a monk and I am a pagan. It would be a traditional thing to mention the divine. Almost expected. "Seek God, my child," that sort of thing. And if you can't say it half way up Mount Sinai, where can you say it? And I don't have to believe you anyway. Indeed, I don't believe you, so you can consider that one settled even now.'

'Well, you're right in a way, of course. Everyone can seek God. But it's not as simple as that. The First Rule of the Spiritual Life states that the extent to which you yield to God is the extent to which you will receive. So there's an element of control there, certainly. That's your thin stick. You can choose to seek or not to seek. And if you seek you will find.'

'So what's the Second Rule of the Spiritual Life?'

'The Second Rule of the Spiritual Life states that the extent to which you yield to God bears no relation to the riches which will be heaped upon you. Seek as much as you like. But in the end, it's up to God to find *you*.'

'So if I'm not much mistaken, the Second Rule of the Spiritual Life is the complete opposite of the First Rule?'

'Indeed. That's the white water of which you spoke. Scary.'

'Typical.'

'Reality.'

I was confused. I was 'Confused of Mount Sinai'. Confused by mystical paths, divine proofs and spiritual rules which did everything except sort anything out.

Confused by the fact that I'd come here to make a quirky programme taking an irreverent and sideways look at a religious shrine, and four days into my visit, had made no progress at all, wasn't feeling at all quirky, and at this particular moment didn't even know where my camera was, for God's sake. Abbot Peter had taken it, saying he knew just the place for it, but he'd left now. So where was it? Where exactly was my security blanket? I eased myself up, so that I was sitting cross-legged. The temperature in the blast furnace was rising. My body ached. I looked down on the monastery buildings below us. We were a little above the rooftops. I felt it was time to return. I felt it was time to do something practical.

'I'd like us to get back to the monastery and find Hatch's parents,' I said. 'They must be very worried.'

'Who are Hatch's parents?'

'I don't know. But I was rather banking on the fact that she might. So I suggest we go and find out.'

Which we duly did. We walked as refugees hobbling home. Faint, but joyful. The candle was re-lit. Comedy was back on the agenda. This was a sort of homecoming. The return of the 'Travellers Two' with adventures to recount around the desert fire and ink-black star-shot sky. We could begin to put things together again. We could find Hatch a big sofa for starters. But by the time we reached the main courtyard, Hatch wasn't thinking about big sofas. Far from it. There was a large crowd gathered. There was disturbance, gasps, consternation, worry, panic. And there was Little's question:

'Why's that man holding my father over the balcony?'

CHAPTER ELEVEN

Concerning the Sofa

WE were being a little careful as we walked down the steps. Partly because of their worn and crumbling condition, partly because of Rowena's worn and crumbling condition, partly because of my rucksack which was more uncomfortable than heavy, and partly because we were looking either side to the rock below.

'It just seems an odd place to put it, that's all,' I said.

'Yes,' said Rowena unconvincingly.

'I mean, why not leave it in the office? It would have been safe there.'

'Yes,' said Rowena again, even more unconvincingly.

'There's something you're not telling me, isn't there?'

'Yes,' said Rowena, returning to more convincing form.

'And that is?'

'Abbot Peter didn't *put* it anywhere. He threw it somewhere.'

'Threw it? Threw my camera?! It's worth thousands of pounds!'

'Not now, it isn't.'

And then I saw it. Or rather I saw some of it. I saw the tripod, bent but obvious and only fifty yards away. I climbed cautiously down from the steps, and across the rocks to where it lay. I sat down next to it. I sat down next to my security blanket of former times. For the rest of what had been my camera lay scattered fairly nearby, smashed, broken, and finished. I picked up and held various pieces of this once slick and clever tool of communication. More technology here than I would ever understand, and I felt a deep sense of awe. It was a remarkable piece of equipment, and a tribute to the extraordinary advances of science; to the extraordinary brains of scientists like the Anorak who had bored me to death at the Feast. Credit where it's due. But demolition is more satisfying.

I looked up at the monastery walls. It had been a long but obviously quick journey down. One heave from Abbot Peter, the silent spinning descent and then the crash and the smash, and the return of the silence. Outside the Tomb he'd told me not to worry about what I found. He'd told me that I was safe. And then he'd taken my camera and thrown it over the cliff. He knew just the place for it, he said. And I'd liked Abbot Peter.

Rowena joined me eventually. The older woman had older legs and older lungs. I took the rucksack off my back. It was rubbing already. I was packed and I was leaving. But I could delay departure a little.

'You saw him throw it?'

'No,' said Rowena, 'but he did mention it in passing. He mentioned that you may be asking for it, and that if you did, just to let you know where it was and that you'd understand. I thought at the time he was a bit optimistic.'

'Maybe. But then again, maybe he was right. I mean, it was fun. Doing TV. It's rather like being paid to look in the mirror. Pennies from heaven for the vain. But it was always a time-filler. While I waited for the truth.'

'Which truth?'

'Oh, I don't know. A truth to dare for, I suppose. That's what Van Gogh said once. He said he wanted to be active in his life, so that when he died he could think, "I'll go where all those who were daring go." And of course by the time he shot himself on that sunny Sunday afternoon, July 27th 1890, he had been active. That's active. So he stumbled back to the inn, bloody, heaving and in pain, but probably happy enough in his restless driven sort of way. The crows over the wheatfield had been calling for a long time, you see. Now finally, he was able to say yes. They called two doctors out. Can't have been easy on Sunday night in Auvers. But after examining him, they decided that the bullet was inaccessible, so they just dressed the wound, level with the edge of the left ribs. He wasn't in serious pain, and his mind seems to have been very clear. He proceeded then to smoke his pipe throughout the night, and when his brother Theo arrived the next day, he told him not to cry, and that he did it for the good of everybody. He died peacefully in Theo's arms at one o'clock in the morning of Tuesday July 29th, aged thirty-seven. His was a daring life. I think he will have gone wherever the daring go.'

'Then I needn't tell you the Fifth Path of the mystics. You are on it already. It is the movement from Action to Intent. It is the movement from the obsession with doing, and being seen to be doing – to the greater calling of knowing what it is that you want, what it is ultimately that you seek. It is about the deep secure longing of intent – and not the surface froth of noticed action. I sense that above all else you intend the truth. That whatever you *do* with your life, or in your life, you intend the truth.'

'In a way I do, Rowena. But it's not as simple as that. I do intend the truth, whatever that means. But it's not just about me, you see.'

'How do you mean?'

'Christians talk about the communion of saints. Those who have gone before.'

'Yes.'

'Well, I have my own communion of saints. My family. My unbelieving family.'

'You feel the weight of their expectation.'

'Yes, I do. But more than that, I want to be with them. I particularly want to be with my dad. And according to you, my dad's in hell.'

*

A while later, I watched Rowena begin the return up the steps. It was slow and it was painful to watch in a way. She was crumbling. They were crumbling. But she knew where she wanted to go. And there's a peace in that, and a peace in seeing it in someone. Step by step by painful step she returned to the truth she'd found. They weren't my steps, of course. They were hers. So what were mine? What were the steps which would lead me to the experience of truth? Had I started the climb? Or was I yet to find my staircase? Rowena believed I had begun to climb, that I was on a path and I was grateful for her belief in me.

Finally, she disappeared round the bend. She didn't look back. She'd said her goodbyes. Gone. And me, alone. Desert child, blinking in the sun. So what was I up for now, while my skies remained free from the beckoning crows? Beneath the action, what did I intend? What was I up for now, till the shades lengthened and evening came for me? The Big Evening. The Final Evening.

I could say my name. I could speak it as Little had done in the cave. But there would have to be strings attached. Big strings, strong strings which could get me back to safety if everything went wrong. No harm in saying it, though. I mean, it seemed childish to me. And there was a large part of me which was saying 'What's the point?' But there again it had an attractive simplicity. The simple telling of my name. And if there was no one out there, who'd lost out? And if there was someone out there? Names matter, after all. I put the tripod down. I felt the space. I felt the turning of the planet. You do when you're on the edge, and I was on every edge going.

And then suddenly from nowhere a plunging loneliness, a terrible darkness and confusion as five generations of atheism loomed and leered at me, confronted and threatened me; as a deep sense of family betrayal jostled me with menace. Like playground bullies who fed on the smeary-teary-eyed, I smelt their breath in my face. I faced them out, cry-eyed but brave, grotesque desert imaginings, snarling at me, 'Teacher's Pet' and 'We'll get you after school.' I believed them. I knew what they did. Paralysed. But I stared them out. I was brave. I was strong. I was good. I'd been through the tunnel. I'd died already. Didn't they realise that? What could they do to me? Didn't they realise that nothing scared me now? There was nothing to dread behind the bike sheds; nothing in the woodshed at the bottom of the garden which I feared. Apart from perhaps love.

Perhaps love. Now there was a fear. Limitless, vulnerable love …

And then nothing. Gone. The grotesque was gone, the distorted disappeared. The sweet breath of stillness. Silence. Desert silence. And my beating heart. But above all, silence, I think. Yes. And above that, peace. Massive peace. Above the silence, peace. And above that, obviously, and indeed beneath it, love.

'My name's Jewel,' I said. I spoke it out loud. 'My name's Jewel. Jenny Jewel. Jewel, as in the precious stone,' I added, maybe unnecessarily. 'Can you hear me, God? Can you hear me, daddy?'

Movement behind. A stone dislodged.

'Who are you talking to?' asked Little.

I was caught out.

'I'm not sure, to be honest. It's something of a three-way conversation, but it's in its early stages. If you see what I mean. Which I doubt you do.'

'I don't.'

'No. Well. Tough.'

I was a little flustered by her arrival. Embarrassed. I didn't need her here right now. I rallied, though.

'Look, I'm sort of practising something.'

'Fine. But when you've finished practising –'

She paused. And looked at me awkwardly.

'I don't think I ever will.'

'It's just that I had a question to ask.'

'And what's that?'

She paused again.

'As questions go, it's quite a big question I suppose.'

'Look, whatever it is, it can't be worse than the Tomb,' I said. 'We've died already, remember?'

Another pause.

'So are you going to take me home, or not?'

'Take you home?'

'With you.'

Shock. Excitement. Impact. A huge alternative future suddenly presented itself.

'Me? Take you home? Well –'

'You mentioned a sofa. A big one.'

'Yes, I did, I did. But I mean –'

'You mentioned it twice.'

'I may have mentioned it twice, Hatch, yes, but –'

'But what?'

But what? But everything! But nothing. A defining moment. A release. A rightness flowed.

'I was just going to say that size isn't everything, Hatch. That's all. You want a big sofa, certainly, but you want one that's the right colour, for instance.'

'That's easy. Yellow. The colour of hope. For the days when I don't feel it.'

'OK. Yellow it is then. A big yellow sofa.'

I adjusted the straps on my rucksack slightly. It was digging.

'Come on,' I said. 'We've got some arranging to do.'

Sorted. She smiled. It was worth the journey. Desert child.

Epilogue

'WELCOME to St James the Less, Archbishop.'

'Musselly, please, Abbot Peter.'

'No baggage?'

'No baggage.'

'Just yourself. And your life.'

'Such as it is.'

'It's awe-inspiring.'

'Not from the inside.'

'And you must, of course, take us, such as we are. Not quite as grand as St Raphael's, I'm afraid. But you will come in?'

'It's not easy.'

'No. Crossing a new threshold. Never easy.'

'You won't ask me to change, will you?'

'What a ridiculous idea.'

'Or demand that I believe more?'

'Please!'

'Or suggest ever so nicely that I try harder?'

'Never.'

'Or demand that I slay my compulsions?'

'Come now!'

'Thank you. Then I might come in.'

With that, Musselly stepped inside the gate. It was a small gate. But it was a big step.

'It is a privilege for us to have you here, Archbishop. Your room is ready. You will do nothing while you are with us, of course. Perhaps later you will do much, but not here. And not now. You will not seek anything, perform anything or intend anything. You will simply accept the fact that you are accepted.'

'Accept that I am accepted? Not easy.'

'No. But very important. It is, in fact, our only rule.'

The two men began to walk across the monastery courtyard. There were some gallows there, but that's another story.

'So we each carry on with what we're doing?' asked Musselly.

'I think so, yes. We carry on as we are, where we are.'

'That's good.'

'Well, prophets, messiahs and other inadequates who rant for revival and hector for change – they're only working out their personal frustrations on the rest of us which is really very tiresome and not to be encouraged either for their sake or ours.'

'Amen.'

'So no, the millennial message is that we carry on as we are, where we are, but that we turn our attention to the Great Possibility, the Grand Miracle, the Massive Moment, the Huge Resurrection.'

'And what's that?'

'That we might actually do what we're doing with a little more kindness.'

Pause.

'That we might actually do what we're doing with a little more kindness?'

Musselly was checking that he had heard aright. Peter, however, confirmed the astounding declaration.

'Indeed. That we might do what we're doing, only with a little more kindness.'

The earth stopped revolving for a moment in shock as the two men considered the implications of the words just spoken; as the two men felt the fall-out from the bombshell just lobbed into the conversation. The visitor spoke first.

'Now that is a very revolutionary thought, my friend.'

'A supremely dangerous muttering, yes, I know. Very dangerous. Not uttered lightly. I was hesitant even as I spoke. The story of the Church has so often been a convincing win for rhetoric over reality. And I really don't want to add to the nonsense. As our Buddhist friends wisely warn, "Don't sell too intoxicating a liquor."'

'Of course. But nevertheless, you think the – er – revolution possible?'

'Well, I feel that it is, yes.'

'Awe-inspiring. Quite awe-inspiring. Imagine it.'

'Sometimes I do, believe me. And it's wonderful.'

The two men smiled at each other, sharing the dangerous secret, and walked on until they reached the large door which said Refectory. They were both clearly still in a state of shock.

'Best not to run before we can walk though,' said the host, eager to calm the almost revivalist fervour unleashed between them.

'Absolutely not. One step at a time.'

'Very important. And the first step at this particular time is, I think, tea.'

'Tea. Very good. Tea should precede every revolution.'

They gazed up through the sky to the universe beyond. It was the visitor who spoke.

'You know something?'

'What?'

'I feel Satan quaking already …'

The kettle was filled. The water was beginning to warm. There was some cake somewhere if Abbot Peter could find it. But first, he needed confirmation.

'So Ted *did* kill himself? He wasn't – er – pushed?'

'He jumped. I've given the whole story to the police.'

'Of course, but as we all know there's the whole story and then there's the whole story. If you see what I mean.'

'It was his decision, not mine. I had been going to drop him. But for some reason I thought better of it. So I'd lifted him back on to the ledge. I was getting tired. He was safe. Safe on that ledge. He seemed relieved. He sat there for a moment, breathing heavily. He looked at me. Almost smiled, I think. But then something inside him turned. He looked at me again. It was different this time. And he said, "Explain this one away, then, with a hundred witnesses down there to call you a liar. You'll wish for the rest of your life you'd followed me." And then he screamed, put his arms in the air, threw himself forward with a vengeance, and –'

'It's all right. I know the rest …'